A HANDFUL OF THIEVES

A HANDFUL OF THIEVES

by

NINA BAWDEN

faber and faber

This edition first published in 2008
by Faber and Faber Ltd
3 Queen Square, London WC1N 3AU

A CIP record for this book is available from the British Library

ISBN 978-0-571-24652-6

CONTENTS

CHAPTER ONE

THE ARRIVAL OF THE SINISTER LODGER

THIS IS THE story of how we became a gang of thieves. My sister Jinny says I shouldn't start like this, giving away the story in the first sentence, but I think she's wrong. If you're writing a book, you've got to make sure the right sort of people read it, haven't you? Otherwise it's not fair to them or to you. So I'm starting off by saying this is a book about thieves and robbers so that no one who would rather read about fairies or magic or talking animals need bother to go any further. It's about me and my friends and how we turned thieves and brought a criminal to justice.

My friends are Rosie, Sid Bates and Algy. We are the ones who really did it all, though some other people helped a bit, like Sid's Uncle William and even Rosie's ghastly friend Clio who we have to put up with because Rosie likes her. My name is Peter Henry McAlpine but I'm always called Fred, I'll explain why later. I am thirteen now, but when this happened I was eleven and two months. My sister Jinny was fourteen then but she doesn't come into the story much except to complain about my grammar and to suggest a different way of putting things, nor do my Mum and Dad. The most important member of my family in this book is my Gran, and as she began it all I had better start with her.

My Gran's name is Edwina Blackadder. She is 'as old as her tongue and a little older than her teeth.' I don't think this is a particularly funny joke—though I did when I was young—but it's what she always says when you ask her how old she is, and as I'm trying to put everything down as it really happened, I'm putting it in. I think she is probably pretty old as she's going bald and her legs are thin as sticks though the rest of her is quite fat. She wears corsets that poke up in front when she sits down.

Her house is in Station Road, near the railway. You don't notice the trains much in the daytime, but at night they shake the doors and rattle things in the cupboards. Mum says it would drive her stark mad living there, she'd never get a wink of sleep, but Gran likes the railway. She says it's company.

Her front room smells of geraniums that she keeps in pots on the window sill. There's a big clock in one corner that ticks very loudly and a rag rug on the floor that I can remember sitting on when I was little and pulling out the loose bits. On the mantelpiece above the fire there is a biscuit barrel with a picture of the Tower of London on the side, a photograph of my grandfather, Albert Blackadder, and a model of Reculver Towers that my Gran bought when she went on her honeymoon to Herne Bay in the old days before the First World War.

My Gran is little, shorter than me, but she had nine brothers who were all over six feet tall. My Mum says she can't think how their parents managed to keep them on a farm labourer's wages, just two children—that's Jinny and me—are expensive enough, heaven knows, but Gran says things were different then. All her brothers are dead now, and my grandfather is dead too: he died before I was born. (My Gran always says 'passed over' but Jinny says 'died' is more accurate and better.) He used to be a picture framer and in the wash-house that leads off the kitchen, there's a stack of carved, gold-coloured frames, some with the old pictures still in them, that he had in stock when he died, and no one's touched since.

'It's time you cleared out that junk, Mother,' my Mum was always saying at one time, when we were there to Sunday tea and she was poking round the kitchen to see how Gran was fixed for groceries. (She usually sent me round the next day with the things Gran was short of, but I thought it was snoopy of her, all the same.) 'You can't possibly use the place with all that stuff cluttering it up, and you never know, Puttock at the Antique Shop might give you a pound or two. All that heavy

Victorian stuff is coming back, though I can't say I care for it myself, it crowds a room.'

'What d'you think I want to use the wash house for? A dance hall?' Gran would say. Or, 'Antiques, my eye! I knew Puttock when he was pushing a barrow round for old iron! All he's got in that shop is the same sort of old rubbish he used to beg in the street for—and a lot of poor silly fools paying good prices for it, what's more. *And* it's tuppence to speak to him! *Good-morning Mrs Blackadder, and how are we today?* Lord Muck in person! As if he thinks I don't remember the time when he was glad to get given a bundle of old rags at my back door! I tell you my girl, I wouldn't demean myself. The day I go crawling to that Puttock for a penny piece I'll be ready for my box, and I'm not ready for that, not by a long chalk.'

(When I was small, I knew 'I'll be ready for my box' was Gran's way of saying she was never going to do something or other, but I didn't understand why. Then Jinny told me it meant 'ready to die and be put in my coffin and buried'. I thought it was a horrid thing to say, but Jinny said it wasn't really: it was just an expression Gran was fond of.)

But most of the time, when Mum told her she ought to get rid of the stuff in the wash-house, Gran would just say nothing. Her mouth would pinch up and she would look cross and obstinate but I could tell she was miserable underneath. I knew how she felt because I'd felt the same sometimes.

My Mum is a great turner-outer. A permanent New Broom, Dad calls her. She used to be always on at me to clear out my cupboard and send all my old toys—my fort and my woolly animals— to the hospital. I could never explain to her why I didn't want to because I wasn't sure why myself. After all, I didn't play with them anymore. But I did find out how to stop her bothering me about it, and that was to keep the door of the cupboard shut, so that whenever she looked into my room she wasn't reminded about the things inside. Mum only thinks about things when she sees them.

Gran must have realized this too, because I saw one day that the wash-house door had a new lock on it. It was a brass Yale lock. Before, there had been an ordinary one with the key always left in, so that anyone could open the door and look in the wash-house whenever they wanted to.

'That's a new lock, isn't it, Gran?' I said.

'New lock, new lock?' she said in an astonished voice, as if I must be soft in the head to suggest such a thing. 'Now, why should I put a new lock on that old door?' Then she winked at me. 'What the eye doesn't see, the heart doesn't grieve over,' she said.

And she kept the wash-house locked after that. I didn't see the door open again, until the day this story really begins. Jinny says I ought to call this chapter 'The Arrival of the Sinister Lodger', and I've done that, although of course we didn't know he was sinister in the beginning. Sid may have said he was, but that was just an inspired guess on his part.

It was a Monday and Sid and I had gone to see Gran on the way home from school, as we often did. My Mum doesn't much like Sid, she says he's a rough character, but Gran says he's a natural gentleman, and always gets down the biscuit barrel when he comes in.

But she didn't this day. In fact, she barely said 'hallo' to us. She was too busy. All the doors were open; from the front room we could see straight through the kitchen and into the wash-house. Everything was upside down and back to front: it was more like coming into my house on one of Mum's turning out days, than into my Gran's. And instead of sitting in her chair by the fire, Gran was halfway up the stairs, struggling with one of the old pictures. It was almost as big as she was, and she was pink in the face and gasping.

'I've got a gentleman coming to see the room,' she explained, stopping to rest for a minute and leaning the picture against the wall.

I was surprised because her last lodger had kept a hamster as a pet. It had got out one night and eaten part of Gran's best bedspread and she'd turned the lodger out next day and said, 'The next time I take a stranger into my house, I'll be ready for my box and I'm not ready for that, not by a long chalk.'

Now she said, 'Mr Puttock asked me. It's his new assistant,' and I was even more surprised, knowing how she felt about old Puttock. Then I thought: maybe she didn't really feel that way after all, only said so, to annoy my Mum. That's the way they always are: anything Mum says, Gran disagrees with, and the other way round. Oil and water don't mix, Dad says, and there you have it.

'I want to make the room look nice,' Gran said. 'I thought I'd put up one of Albert's pictures. But it's heavier than I thought.'

'Igiyuan,' Sid said, which means, 'I'll give you a hand.' From now on, I'll write what Sid says in translation, because otherwise it's too tiring to read.

'Thank you, Sid,' Gran said. 'I'm sure a picture will brighten the room up a bit.'

What the room really needed wasn't 'brightening', but to be made at least ten times bigger. It was so crammed full of enormous furniture that it looked more like a removal van than a bedroom. There was a huge brass bed, two tall wardrobes, a dressing table with a swing mirror, several other ordinary tables with pot plants standing on them and a big treadle sewing machine that Gran had had ever since she trained to be a dressmaker, when she was young. To get round the bed, you had to turn sideways and walk like a crab.

'He'll have to be a pretty thin lodger,' I said, as Sid and I wriggled between the bed and the wardrobes, clutching the heavy old picture between us.

'Thin or fat, he'll be glad to have a roof over his head and some decent furniture to look at and put his things in,' Gran said sharply. 'It's all good stuff, let me tell you. Not like some of that gimcrack muck people put up with nowadays, fall apart as soon as look at it!'

'We'll have to geton the bed to get the picture up,' Sid said. 'Got a bit of newspaper, Mrs B?'

Gran put some newspaper on the bed and we climbed on to it. Sid took his shoes off first, but I forgot. It wasn't easy to get the picture up because there was a feather mattress on the bed and we lurched about, sinking into it and trying to keep our balance, but we managed in the end. When the picture was hooked on the picture rail, we got down and had a look at it.

It was a fattish lady lying on a sofa. She looked as if she ought to be in bed, because she was wearing a nightdress, but the sofa was out of doors: there were trees at the back and sheep and a goat skipping round in front. The nightdress was the kind you can see through, and when Sid saw this he gave a stifled giggle and glanced at me sideways, but I pretended not to notice: old pictures are often like that and it's not rude, just Art. 'It's a nice picture, Gran,' I said, to make up for saying what I had about the room being too crowded for a lodger, though I thought, privately, that it was a silly sort of picture to hang in a grown man's bedroom.

Gran sighed and wiped her hands on her apron. 'Albert always liked it. Can't say I do myself, but at least it's a good frame,' she said. 'Gilt.'

She put the bedcovers straight and Sid got his shoes on. Then we went downstairs and helped put the furniture back and Sid fetched a scuttle of coal. The fire danced up the chimney and the room became hot as a furnace. Gran took off her apron and took two small glasses and a bottle of her home made wine out of the cupboard. 'Plum,' she said, 'strictly non-alcoholic,' and winked at me because the last time she had given me a glass—damson, that time—Mum had made a fuss when I told her, saying it wasn't suitable for a boy my age. 'Least said, soonest mended,' Gran said now, and I winked back and sipped at my drink, making it last because I knew I wouldn't get a second one. Sid drained his off in a gulp and then reeled about, pretending to be drunk, until Gran said, 'Get along with you, Sid Bates, what you've had wouldn't intoxicate a fly.'

'I've got a much weaker constitution than a fly,' Sid said, and collapsed on to the sofa, rolling his eyes. Sid never talks to grown-ups in the ordinary way. If they speak to him, he just stands, hanging his head and answering in grunts, but when we're with Gran he chats away and acts the fool the way he does when we're alone together. Though he talks so badly, running his words together, Sid is really the cleverest of our lot, probably because he's so much smaller: while the rest of us have been busy growing, all Sid's energy has been going into his brain.

'You need building up, then,' Gran said. She went into the kitchen and came back with a plate of ham sandwiches, cut in triangles with the crusts off, and a bit of parsley for decoration. 'Just one each, now, and don't drop the crumbs.' She sat down in her chair and rocked for a bit and then looked at the clock. 'He's coming about quarter past five,' she said, and I knew she was hoping we'd be gone by then and that the ham sandwiches were really for the lodger. I felt rather jealous, suddenly.

'Is he going to pay you a lot of money, Gran?' I asked.

'Ask no questions and you'll be told no lies,' she said. Then she smiled. 'Enough to keep the wolf from the door, Paul Pry.'

(Gran never talked about money, but I knew she only had her old age pension to live on and that it wasn't really enough, because Mum and Dad sometimes discussed it. Dad said they ought to make her an allowance but Mum thought it was more sensible to give her a few groceries and a sack of coal from time to time. 'There's no point in giving her money, she'd only give it away to someone else. I know my mother, she'd give the shirt off her back to any Tom, Dick or Harry who asked for it,' Mum said. Dad argued a bit, but he always loses the arguments in our house, and Mum finished this one by saying, 'I bet she's got a bit put by anyway.' Mum only said this to have the last word, but it was true, in fact: Gran had forty-five pounds in five pound notes in an old teapot on the dresser in the kitchen. I'd found the money when I was looking for a bit of string for conkers, and she said she was keeping it for a rainy day. I asked her why she didn't put it in the Post Office or a bank, and she said she didn't trust the Government. 'Only for the Lord's sake, don't tell your Mother. I'd never hear the last of it,' she said.)

'Can't we stay and see the lodger, Gran?' I asked, but Sid frowned at me.

He got up from the sofa and said, very politely, 'Thank you for the ham sandwich and the liquid refreshment, Mrs B. They have amply sustained my Inner Man.' He clicked his heels and bowed and Gran laughed. Sid could always make her laugh.

'It was my pleasure, Mr Bates,' she said. 'Any time you're passing . . .'

She kissed me goodbye and we went out. It was a little after five by this time, and, as we walked up the street, we saw a man in a raincoat coming towards us. The raincoat was much too big for him, dangling over his wrists and flapping round his legs. He was carrying a suitcase and looking at the numbers of the houses. I nudged Sid and we ambled along, whistling under our breath and occasionally jumping the cracks in the paving stones, but taking a good look as we got close. He glanced in our direction but only in the casual way grown-ups often do: they look at children without really *seeing* them, which is something that comes in useful later on in this story.

But we saw him all right. Descriptions of people are often boring, but it is important to describe the lodger. He was a thin man with a thin, pale face and a long nose that seemed to quiver as he walked, rather like an ant-eater's snout or a cat's whisker. And he looked, somehow, terribly sad. I thought at the time that it was just because he was looking for Gran's house and was afraid he wasn't going to find it, but when I saw him afterwards he looked just the same: lost and mournful with brown eyes that were always damp as if he had only that minute stopped crying.

'Looks as if he could do with those ham sandwiches, don't he?' Sid whispered.

We dodged across the road and trailed him back to make sure he really was the lodger, and hid behind a parked van. He pushed open Gran's squeaky gate and walked up the front path. Gran must have been watching behind the curtain because she opened the door at once and we heard her say, 'Mr Gribble is it? I'm so pleased to see you.' I peered round the van. He was very tall and she looked little and bent beside him.

'Gribble's the name. I am honoured to make your acquaintance, my dear Mrs Blackadder.' He had a deep, thrilling voice like a foghorn. 'It's good of you to take in a weary wanderer like myself. A true act of Christian charity.'

'Not at all, Mr Gribble,' Gran said. 'You're very welcome . . .'

'And I am more than grateful, dear lady.' Mr Gribble bowed his head as if he were about to pray. 'I trust I shall be no great burden to you,' he boomed. 'My wants are simple, Mrs Blackadder. I am a simple man . . .'

'I'm sure we shall get on very well, Mr Gribble,' Gran said. 'Won't you come in?'

'I shall be happy to enter your hospitable portals, ma'am.' Mr Gribble didn't sound happy, more as if he were about to burst into tears, and he made no move to go indoors. He set his suitcase down and lifted his head to look at the front of the house. 'Be it never so humble, there's no place like home. That's what I often say, Mrs Blackadder.'

'Do come in, Mr Gribble.' Gran spoke quite tartly. Perhaps she thought it was rude of him to describe her house as humble, or perhaps she was afraid he might stand on her doorstep for the rest of the evening, keeping her out in the cold and making long, windy speeches.

When the front door had closed, Sid and I looked at each other.

'What a pompous ass,' I said. 'On and on . . . Just like old Thuggins.' (Old Thuggins is our headmaster.)

Sid was silent a minute. Then he said, unexpectedly, 'I don't think he's like old Thuggins. Old Thuggins is just a fool. But this man Gribble, well, it sounded to me as if he was just pretending to be one. As if he was *acting*. If you ask me, I think he's *sinister*.'

'Don't be daft,' Sid has got what our English master calls a good imagination, which means that he often makes things out to be more complicated than they really are. I said, 'He sounds a ghastly drip, an absolutely awful *bore*, and I should think he'll drive Gran stark staring mad but what's sinister about him?'

'Oh, I dunno.' Sid's round pink face went pinker still. 'It's the way he talks somehow. It's not natural. I mean, for one thing, that's a *fat man's voice*.'

'Oh don't be a nit,' I said.

CHAPTER TWO

THE CEMETERY COMMITTEE

AFTER HELPING GRAN and hanging about to wait for the lodger, we were late at the Cemetery. We belted along as fast as we could, down the cinder path at the side of the station yard, but by the time we got to Death Wall, Algy was waiting for us, although he'd already been home, after school, and had his tea.

Death Wall is the steep side of an old motor racing track that's been abandoned for years and years; the concrete has cracked open and there are bushes growing up through the cracks, but there are enough smooth patches left to get a good, frightening ride on the pram wheels we picked up on the dump. There's an aircraft factory on the far side of the track where the spectators' stands used to be, but most of the site is just a dump with a weedy river running through it. It belongs to the factory and there is barbed wire all round and notices saying 'No Admittance For Unauthorised Persons', but we have a private way in, up through the brambles on the railway embankment to a gap in the wire at the top of the Wall. It's known as Death Wall because so many racing motorists used to be killed there, and at the bottom of the slope, which we call the cemetery, there's a wonderful pile of old cars. Most of them are wrecked racing cars of course, but among them there's an enormous old Humber saloon with leather seats. The doors have come off now and someone has pinched the steering wheel, but at the time I'm writing about, it was still fairly solid: we could keep good and dry there, except when it rained very hard.

It was beginning to spit when we pushed through the brambles and Algy was sitting on the top of the Wall, huddled under his cycling cape and looking miserable.

'I came to say I can't come,' he said, which is a typical Algy remark. I started to point out that it didn't make sense, since here he was, but Sid cut in—quite rightly, because it's a waste of time trying to make Algy logical—and asked him why.

'Homework,' Algy said, with an expression of deep gloom. 'My parents say I'm not working hard enough.'

Most parents have their difficult side, but Algy's parents are awful all round. At least, they were at that time. Sid was at the top of the A stream in Milton High School and I was halfway down, but Algy was in the C stream and his mother and father seemed to think this was not only a terrible, personal disgrace, but a wicked plot on the part of the Government or something. It was bad enough that they bullied Algy about it, but what was much worse, they wrote letters to the school which let Algy in for a lot of sarcastic comment from his form master, who wasn't the nicest man at the best of times. It was really unfair because Algy couldn't help being dim and his parents never seemed to notice the things he was good at, like mending bicycles and electric motors, nor to see what a nice person he was. Dim but decent and dogged, Sid says, which is just a way of saying Algy's the sort of person you can absolutely rely on, who would never let you down. There is that saying about the king who 'never said a stupid thing and never did a wise one.' Well, with Algy, it's more or less the other way round.

'They say if I don't pull my socks up, I'll never get into university,' Algy said.

'Do you want to? All that beastly *work?*' I said, though I knew, really, that what Algy wanted didn't come into it.

Algy knew it too. The rain was splashing on his spectacles, his spiky hair stood on end, and he looked pale and desperate. 'My mother says if I don't get into Oxford in six years time it'll break my father's heart.'

Sid thumped him in the back. 'Cheer up, you may be dead before then.'

'No such luck.' Algy shook his head but the thought seemed

to give him a gleam of hope and he looked a bit less dejected. 'I've got to be back by six-thirty sharp,' he said, 'so I've got about an hour.'

It was beginning to rain hard now, so there was no point in racing on the pram wheels: we skidded down the concrete slope towards the Humber. As we scrambled into the musty-smelling inside of the car, Sid gave a squeal and clutched my arm. For a minute he looked quite scared; then he laughed and collapsed on to the back seat. 'Oh, my poor heart.'

'You feminine *nit*,' I said. 'It's only Aristotle.'

Aristotle was the guy we were making for Firework Day. Propped up in the front seat of the Humber, a tweed hat jammed down on his head, he looked just like a man sitting there. He had an old jacket of my Dad's, trousers stuffed with newspaper balls, and a marvellous *papier-maché* mask Rosie had made, with hollow white cheeks and a lumpy, red, drunkard's nose. He was almost finished now; all he needed was a stitch or two and some wool for his hair.

'Rosie's bringing the wool this evening,' Sid said. 'So we'll have to wait till she comes. Shall we check over the Fund?'

The Fund was in a tin box under the back seat. We got it out and counted it for something to do, though we knew the amount by heart. Fifteen shillings and threepence-halfpenny and only two weeks to Firework Day.

'Three decent rockets, a few squibs and a couple of Roman Candles, and that's just about our lot,' Sid said.

I dug in my pocket. 'I've got one and six left of my pocket money.'

Algy pulled a face. 'No good looking at me. I got rotten marks in my maths last week.'

Algy got ten shillings a week, four times as much as I did, but his parents being what they were, he could never rely on it.

'We'd better start giving you a hand with your homework,' Sid said drily, and put ninepence into the tin himself. In fact,

Sid had more money than any of us—he did a paper round and sometimes swept up in the supermarket on Saturday mornings—but his mother's a widow and has rheumatism, so he gave her most of it.

'You need about five pounds to get a decent lot of fireworks,' I said. 'They've gone up like everything else. It's the cost of living. My Mum says the Government ought to do something.'

'Free fireworks for all,' Sid said. 'It's quite an idea. But we ought to get a bit more if we push Aristotle round on the pram. He's a pretty good guy.'

'Old Thuggins said we weren't to,' Algy reminded him. This was true: the pompous ass had given us a long lecture in Assembly the other morning, braying on and on about how he 'trusted—nay sincerely *believed*—that no pupil of Milton High would be seen annoying people in the street by asking for a Penny For The Guy.'

'So long as we don't wear school uniform, I can't see it matters,' I said.

'He said it would be letting down the School. He put us on our *honour*,' Algy said, going stubborn the way he often does on a point like this. Of course, we argued with him, explaining that you can't put people on their honour unless they agree to it, or are at least given a chance to discuss the matter—which with old Thuggins no one ever is—but Algy dug in his heels and was getting quite white in the face, he was so worked up about it, when we heard Rosie's whistle.

Sid wound down the window which was steamed up inside, and stuck out his head to whistle back. Then he said, 'Oh Lord, guess what! The dreaded Clio is with her. Stuck up on the wall and squealing!'

Algy and I groaned.

Sid said in a shrill voice, 'Oh, I can't possibly get down that dweadful steep slope, I'm so scared, poor little me,' and he sounded so much like Clio that by the time Rosie opened the door of the Humber, Algy and I were in fits, rolling round on the seat and clutching our stomachs.

'Share the joke, can't you?' Rosie tried to look puzzled, though she knew quite well what we were laughing at, as she knew quite well how we felt about Clio. And, in case it seems as if we were being unkind, I should explain that we didn't mind Rosie making a new friend now she had gone to her new school—we had all been together at the Primary, and she was probably pretty lonely without us—but she had no business to bring Clio down to the Cemetery, which was our private place, without asking the Committee's permission first. Rosie was perfectly aware that she was in the wrong, and so of course she started attacking us.

'I think you're horribly mean and foul, laughing at Clio. And not just foul to *her*. It's foul to *me*. Why shouldn't I have another girl on the Committee? It was me found this place in the beginning, wasn't it? You'd never have thought of coming here, not in a million years! Why shouldn't I bring someone along, if I want to?'

We said nothing. Rosie in a rage is enough to silence anyone. She glared at us for a minute, looking like an angry witch with her black hair streaked round her brown face and her brown eyes snapping. Then she said, in a quieter voice, 'And anyway, you ought to be pleased! I told her she could probably join the Committee if she put some money into the Fund and so we went to her house on the way home and she's got fifteen shillings.'

'Oh,' I said. 'Well, in *that* case . . .'

'Shut up, Fred,' Algy said crossly. 'The money doesn't matter. Rosie's right. It's only fair, really. I mean, if she *wants* another girl . . .'

We turned to Sid. He was grinning and there was a devilish gleam in his eye. 'All right then,' he said. 'All right, Rosie, you win. Tell her to come on down and meet the Committee.'

Rosie looked embarrassed.

'Go on,' Sid urged. 'Give her a shout.'

Rosie's cheeks went red. 'She's scared of the Wall.' We all lay back on the seats of the Humber and stared at the roof. If we'd looked at each other, we'd have died laughing. 'I know it sounds silly, but it *is* awfully steep and scarey,' Rosie said— Rosie, who went down that slope on the pram wheels faster than anyone! None of us spoke and she went on, pleading quite humbly now, 'And it's not just that she's scared, she thinks you don't want her, too. Won't you come up and talk to her? Just this once? I'll get her down the Wall next time, I promise.'

We sat up, feeling ashamed. At least I did, and I think Sid did too because he didn't glance at me or Algy as he got out of the car and followed Rosie across the dump to the Wall. He was able to run straight up the slope because he had studs on his shoes. The rest of us climbed up more slowly, zig-zagging backwards and forwards and clutching at the scrubby bushes when we came to an extra slippery bit: the concrete is treacherous in the wet.

Sid was talking to Clio who was sitting on the Wall. The rain had stopped and it was growing dusk: Clio's hair stood out against the inky sky like a candle flame. She has yellow hair, the colour of a duckling's feathers, blue eyes, pink cheeks and a silly, simpering smile of which we got the full benefit as we panted up to the top.

Sid says I can join your gang,' she said, tossing back her hair to make sure we noticed how much there was of it, and letting out a high, giggly laugh.

It was important to put her in her place from the beginning. 'It's not a gang,' I said. 'We're not babies. It's a Committee. The Cemetery Committee.'

'Ooo—I think that sounds *gruesome*.' She pronounced it 'gwoosome', widening her eyes so that they looked like enormous blue marbles, and pretending to shiver.

'You don't have to join it then,' I said hopefully.

'But Rosie said I could. And I brought fifteen shillings for

the Fund.' Her lower lip started trembling as if she were going
to cry. I was almost sure she was acting, but just in case she
wasn't I said quickly, 'Okay, then, you can join if you want.
But you've got to understand that if you put your fifteen
shillings into the Fund it doesn't belong to you any more, it
belongs to the Committee and we all agree what it's to be
spent on.'

'Fireworks, this time of the year,' Sid said. 'Afterwards,
we're going to save up for a canoe.'

She gave him a sharp look. 'You can't buy fireworks. You
have to be over fourteen. It's the law.'

'Algy's tall enough to pass,' Sid said.

She looked at Algy. 'All right, then. As long as we all have
a say in what he buys. I don't want a lot of nasty bangers.' She
gave her stupid giggle again: it sounded like the bath water
running out. 'I know what you boys are!'

She said 'boys' as if they were some rather beastly species
of animal. It made me mad. I said, 'There's one thing you have
to do before you join the Committee, though. You have to run
down the Wall.'

She was quiet a minute, looking down the slope. She said,
under her breath, 'Oh *no* . . .' and there was a little catch in her
voice, which wasn't put in for effect. To be fair, the slope did
look alarming in the half dark, steeper even than it was, and
with a lot of menacing, black shapes at the bottom. They were
only old bits of machinery turned out of the aircraft factory at
one time or another, but she couldn't be expected to know that.
'Rosie,' she said, 'do I have to?'

Rosie looked uncomfortable, as well she might: it was she
who had thought up this particular rule when we formed the
Committee and she should have warned Clio beforehand.

'It's not as bad as it looks,' she said. 'There's only one really
rough bit you have to watch out for. Where Algy fell and
broke two front teeth and his glasses.'

Clio didn't seem to find this much comfort. The simpering

grin had gone from her face and she looked blank and frightened.

Algy said suddenly, 'She needn't really, need she? Not tonight.'

'It's in the rules,' I said. 'Isn't it, Sid?'

Sid cleared his throat and nodded.

'It doesn't say anything about doing it in the dark,' Algy said.

'Oh, all *right*.' I turned to Clio. 'You can do it tomorrow in the daylight, then. Okay?'

She stared at me for a minute without any expression at all. Then she said, surprising us all, I think, 'No. If I've got to do it sometime, I'd rather get it over with.'

And before we could tell her which way to go to avoid the worst patches, she was off. It's not, in fact, as dangerous as it looks, because although the steepness at the top is frightening even when you are used to it, the slope flattens out near the bottom and as long as you're not clumsy, like Algy, and you don't bang into any of the machinery, you get down without breaking any bones. Clio ran down safely enough, she was light and sure on her feet, but at the bottom she keeled over as if she'd been shot, and lay screaming, a high, thin shriek like a train whistle.

'Oh *Christmas*,' Sid said, and went down after her. Rosie and I followed. I felt pretty scared, as you can imagine, but she hadn't hurt herself, just tumbled down from fright and grazed her knee. Sid was dabbing at it with his handkerchief and saying, 'Shush now, it's not bad,' as if she were a baby. Then, when she didn't stop, he added savagely, 'Shut *up* can't you? D'you want old Puffer to hear?'

Old Puffer was the night watchman. We called him Puffer because of the way he breathed, in and out like a pair of wheezy bellows. Sometimes he came by on his rounds while we were in the Humber and we lay quiet till he'd passed. He came on duty when the factory closed at five o'clock and went round the site about an hour later.

'It's about six now,' I said, horrified. 'Do belt up, Clio, he'll hear you.'

She stopped at the top of a scream, hiccuped, and stood quiet. But it was too late. Algy shouted from the top of the Wall, 'Watch out, the Committee,' and there was old Puffer, weaving his way through the machinery at the bottom of the track, his torch jumping about like a will-o-the-wisp as he yelled at us. 'Stop where y'are now, d'you hear? I want a word with you.'

'I can't run, my breath's gone,' Clio said, teetering helplessly between Sid and me.

'Used it up screaming, you half wit,' I said. 'Here—catch on to me.'

'I'll take her, I've got my boots,' Sid said, and went up the slope like a maniac, dragging Clio behind him. Rosie and I followed more slowly: we were a bit scared but not *very* scared because Puffer's bark was worse than his bite. He'd chased us off once or twice before, but only as a sort of game. 'You'll get a good hiding if I catch you,' he grumbled now, making his way diagonally across the slope as if to cut us off, but he wasn't really trying very hard. He had to put up a bit of a show because it was his job, but I don't think he actually minded us being on the site as long as we didn't thrust ourselves under his nose. Several times, when we'd been hiding from him in the Humber, I'd got the idea that he knew we were there and was deliberately looking the other way.

It was Clio who changed this situation. On the top of the wall, and excited, I suppose, because she was safe, she suddenly screamed out, 'Silly old fool. Silly, fat, puffing old fool.'

Which was not only rude but stupid, too, because old Puffer changed his attitude at once. He couldn't catch us— though there was one nasty moment when Rosie slipped back down the slope and I had to get hold of her and haul her up— but when he reached the top and we were crashing down through the brambles, the tone of his voice was quite different.

'You come back here again and I'll tan the hide off you, I'll report you to the police,' he shouted, and we could tell that this time he meant it. Now we had insulted him, we wouldn't be safe if he caught us.

He was too old to get down the embankment after us, but we ran as if he could.

'You are a fool, Clio,' Sid gasped, as we reached the cinder path. 'Whatever made you say that? Honestly, you haven't got the brains you were born with!'

'We won't be able to go there again, not ever!' I said, not because I really believed this, but to bring home to Clio what she had done.

Winded, we slowed to a trot and then to a walk. Clio began to snivel. Rosie put an arm round her shoulders and glared indignantly at Sid and me. 'Don't take any notice of them, Clio,' she said, 'they're just being mean.' But the stupid girl went on snivelling.

No one spoke again until we got to the railway sidings before the station yard. Then Algy said, 'We'll have to go back. There's the Fund and we'll have to rescue Aristotle.'

'We'd better wait a few days,' Sid said, and grinned at me. 'Give old Puffer time to simmer down.'

CHAPTER THREE

HUBBEL'S FLUID

As it turned out, the Committee didn't meet at Death Wall again until the end of that week, though not for any strategic reason to do with old Puffer. The weather was so awful. Not just drizzle and damp but pelting rain that danced on the pavements. Even if it had not been for his precious Homework, Algy wouldn't have been allowed out in the evening in case he caught a cold, and Sid's mother got rheumatism so badly that he had to stay at home to look after her. I saw Rosie once, outside Woolworth's but she stuck her nose in the air and pretended not to notice me. I guessed she was still angry with me on Clio's behalf.

So I was stuck with my family. I wouldn't have minded in the ordinary way; as familys go, mine are not bad at all, but this week there was something of an atmosphere in the house. Mum was annoyed because Gran had taken a lodger. It was really because Gran hadn't asked her advice first, but that wasn't the reason she gave.

'It *looks* so bad,' was what she said on Friday. She and I were playing chess, Jinny was washing her hair upstairs and Dad was reading by the fire. No one had mentioned Gran that particular evening, but Dad and I knew what Mum was talking about: she had talked about nothing else for days. 'As if she needed the money,' she went on, so distracted by this thought that she put her king in check and I had to point it out to her.

'As if she hadn't got a family to help her!'

'She has, but we don't much, do we?' Dad said. He coughed and leaned forward in his chair to tap out his pipe on the side of the fireplace.

'How many times have I told you not to do that?' Mum

cried, and almost upset the chessboard in her hurry to fetch a dustpan and brush.

While she was out of the room, Dad winked at me. 'It's a sort of private war between your mother and the forces of nature,' he said. 'I'm surprised that she doesn't dust the coal before she brings it in.'

But if he had hoped to take Mum's mind off Gran, he hadn't succeeded. On her hands and knees, brushing away as if Dad had dropped a bag of soot in the hearth instead of a little bit of tobacco, she said, 'I don't like it, I can't pretend I do. She's got enough to do at her age, looking after herself without waiting hand and foot on that great, solemn fool of a man! She'll knock herself up and then what'll happen, I ask you? I said to her this afternoon, *Mother, you'll wear yourself out*, and she said, *If I do, it's none of your business, my girl*. None of my business, I like that! Who does she think is going to look after her if she takes to her bed? I tell you, I think one of the reasons she took this man Gribble, is that she knew it would annoy *me*.'

'That's not true, Mum,' I said. 'She took him because Mr Puttock asked her.'

'And why should she do what Puttock wants, may I ask? She can't stand the sight of him, if she's told me that once, she's told me a hundred times.'

Dad said soothingly, 'Well, it's not Puttock she's got staying, is it? It's this man Gribble.'

'And who's he, that's what I'd like to know?' Mum sat back on her heels and waved the brush threateningly at Dad and me. 'No one's seen him round here before. It's typical of my mother to take in someone she doesn't know the first thing about. A stranger *and* a vegetarian, too!'

'Neither is exactly a crime.' Dad looked as if he were trying not to laugh.

I said, 'He's not so bad, really Mum. And it's nice for Gran to have company.'

I said this to stick up for Gran, though I didn't like Mr
Gribble much myself. And though there wasn't, as Dad said,
any crime in being a vegetarian, he did make an awful song and
dance about it.

I had heard him. The first time I had met him properly was
Tuesday. Mum hadn't seen him then, or spoken to Gran since
he arrived, but though she complained that the whole thing
had been arranged behind her back, she still sent me round to
Gran's with a beautiful piece of steak. 'She'll want something
nice for his supper,' she said.

When I got to Gran's house, they were sitting on either side
of the fire. Mr Gribble had his shoes off and his feet were
propped up on a stool. There was a huge hole in the toe of one
sock. There was a pot of tea on the table, and the room
looked very cosy.

I gave Gran the steak. Blood was seeping through the parcel.
I saw Mr Gribble looking at it, so I said, 'It's a nice piece of
rump steak. My Mum thought you'd like it.'

He closed his eyes and a shudder seemed to go through him.
Then he looked at Gran and put up one hand like a policeman
stopping the traffic. 'Not for me, Mrs Blackadder,' he boomed
in his deep, foghorn voice. 'You know my views.'

Gran went a bit pink, and took the meat out to the kitchen.
Mr Gribble looked at me mournfully. 'I never touch animal
products, young man. Only the natural food of the earth—
whole wheat, nuts and fruit. Nature has given us her bounty.
Don't you think we should be grateful, and not ask for
more?'

I could think of no answer to this, so I said nothing.

He beckoned to me with a long, white, boney finger and I
went over to his chair. He took my hand; his felt cold and a
little slimy, but it seemed rude to pull away. 'What's your
name, boy?'

'McAlpine, Sir,' I said. 'P. H. McAlpine. But I'm called

Fred. Fred spelt with a Ph, see?' This was a joke of my Dad's, but Mr Gribble didn't seem to find it funny: he just gazed and gazed at me with his sad, damp eyes as if he were seeing into my mind. I said, to distract his attention from me, 'Can I get you another cup of tea, sir?'

'Mr Gribble doesn't drink tea, he believes it inflames the passions,' Gran said, coming back into the room.

She looked at me, very straight-faced.

I glanced at the tea pot on the table and she said, rather defiantly, 'Oh, I'm afraid it's no good trying to teach *me* new habit's now!'

'And I wouldn't presume to try, dear Mrs Blackadder,' Mr Gribble said gallantly. 'Live and let live, that's my motto. Which is why I prefer to see the little lambs gambolling in the field, rather than roasting in my oven. I take no credit for my attitude, mind. I was simply fortunate to be born with a spiritual nature and a very sensitive palate. I have always taken care not to blunt it with tea, coffee or alcohol.' He took a steaming mug from the table beside him and sipped at it slowly. Then he said, with his sad, sad smile, 'I hope I have not put you off your tea, dear lady.'

'Indeed you haven't!' Gran said. She picked up her cup, looked at it, then put it down as if she didn't fancy it after all and stared into the fire. The rolling echo of Mr Gribble's voice died away and the room suddenly seemed very quiet. The only sounds were the tick of the clock in the corner and the wet smack of Mr Gribble's lips as he drank whatever he had in his mug.

Suddenly, I longed to know. 'What are you drinking, sir?' I asked.

He smacked his lips once more, in a reflective way. 'I am drinking Hubbel's Fluid, young man. An excellent beverage made from wheat husks, peanuts and molasses. Perhaps you would like to join me?'

I could hardly say no. I said yes, please, I would love to. Gran gave me a doubtful look, but she fetched a cup and Mr Gribble took a jar that stood on a small table beside him. He unscrewed the lid and put a spoonful of what looked like brown dust into the cup. He poured in hot water from the kettle on the hearth, stirred the mixture and handed it to me.

'There my boy,' he said. 'A fine, natural drink from earth's garden, suitable to man's nature and his needs.'

A slightly fishy smell rose up from the cup, but not bad enough to be a proper warning. I took a mouthful—and nearly spat it out. It was horrible, the most horrible muck I had ever tasted. Thick, sticky, with a dreadful seaweedy taste—it was just like drinking a fishy glue.

I looked at Gran but she looked away. Gran is a very unfussy person in many ways but she has very strict ideas about good manners. Since I had asked for the Hubbel's Fluid, and Mr Gribble believed he was giving me a treat, I knew she would expect me to drink it.

I managed to get down about half and in spite of feeling sick I was pretty proud of myself. when Gran said, 'Let me taste it, will you? I never have.' And before I could speak she almost snatched the cup from my hand and drained it. When she had finished, she looked rather ill and shaken, but her eyes were twinkling at me. 'I'm so sorry, Fred. Was that terribly greedy?'

'That's all right, Gran,' I said. I wanted to hug her, but I was afraid that if I did, Mr Gribble would know why, so I just sat still and grinned back at her.

'If the whole world drank Hubbel's Fluid,' Mr Gribble said, 'it would be a happier, more peaceful place. Ah—you may smile, Mrs Blackadder, but what is it that causes war? Anger and passion. Hubbel's Fluid calms down this baser side of man's nature. I tell you truthfully, when I have partaken of a mug or two I am filled with good will to all mankind.'

And he lay back in his chair, folded his thin hands across his chest and closed his eyes.

Gran saw me to the door. She closed it behind us and we stood outside on the step. She whispered, 'He's right in one way, Fred. If people drank that muck all the time, they'd be feeling much too sick to start a war or any old nonsense like that.' I giggled and she went on, more seriously, 'But he's a good man, you know, in spite of his funny ways. He worries about the world, it makes me quite sad to hear him sometimes. And he gives all his money away.'

'Who to?'

'Oh—poor people. Widows and orphans,' Gran said—rather vaguely, I thought. 'All I know is, he hasn't a penny piece to bless himself with, poor man. It's a nice change to meet someone so unselfish, it makes me quite ashamed, sometimes.'

I met Sid in the High Street on Saturday morning. His mother was better, he said. He would be back at school next week.

'That lodger of Gran's,' I told him. 'He's not sinister at all, just crazy as a coot. You should hear him, he thinks no one should eat anything except nuts and fruit and you should just taste that muck he drinks.' My stomach turned over as I thought of it. 'Oh my Lord,' I said.

'He eats meat sometimes,' Sid said.

'What d'you mean? 'Course he doesn't. He's a vegetarian.'

'I saw him,' Sid said. 'Down at the café next to Woolworth's the other day. Tucking into a plate of steak and chips.'

'You *couldn't* have!'

Sid shrugged his shoulders. 'Call me a liar then, I don't mind.'

'No. I just mean it must have been someone else.'

'I don't think so.' Sid looked thoughtful. 'Though he did have his back to the light.'

It seemed odd: Mr Gribble wasn't the sort of man you could easily mistake. But there were more important things to talk about, so we decided that Sid must have been wrong, and got on with them.

The rain had stopped and it was fine and bright: a good day for Death Wall. The factory closed at lunch-time on Saturday; the best time to go would be about three o'clock when old Puffer would be brewing up tea in his shed on the far side of the site. Rosie lived in Larchmont Grove which was on Sid's way home and I said—rather nobly, because this was a job neither of us cared for—that I'd get hold of Algy.

I telephoned him when I got home and of course his mother answered. Getting on to Algy direct was about as easy as trying to speak to the Queen. His mother wanted to know who I was and what I wanted him for.

'Just to come out this afternoon, tell him it's Fred,' I said.

'Well, Fred, I don't know that he can.' She had one of those *haw-haw* voices, as if she were speaking with a golf ball in her mouth. 'I'm not sure that he's free.'

'Can I speak to him, then?'

There was a short silence. She said, grudgingly, 'I think he's in his room, but he may be busy. I can't disturb him if he's doing his homework, you know.'

'I wouldn't want to *disturb* him,' I said. 'But I'd like to speak to him for a minute, if he can spare the time.' I had to be polite, for Algy's sake.

She fetched him then, but she waited by the telephone while Algy spoke. I could tell by his buttoned-up voice. 'That you, Fred?'

'No, it's the Lord Mayor of London,' I said. 'Is that the Duke of Edinburgh? I'm sorry to disturb you, Your Royal Highness, but the Committee assembles this afternoon, fifteen hundred hours. The Archbishop of Canterbury and President Johnson will be there. Will it be convenient for Your Majesty to be present?'

'I think so.' I could hear his mother hissing away in the background like a distrustful snake, then Algy's whispered answer.

'Only out for a bike ride, mother. No, nowhere dangerous. Yes, I promise.'

'Just the dead centre of the town—the Cemetery,' I said. I gave a hollow, menacing laugh, and put down the receiver.

CHAPTER FOUR

THE SAD END OF ARISTOTLE

THE FINE WEATHER held. We had a good half hour on the pram wheels while we judged old Puffer was busy with his tea. Two of us held the wheels steady at the top of the slope while the one whose turn it was, got into position; although it was more alarming to lie on your stomach, you were less likely to come a cropper. Even Clio took her turn, though it was clearly more of a duty than a pleasure, and Rosie exceeded her own speed record: five seconds flat by Algy's stop watch. Five seconds meant that she couldn't brake with her feet halfway down as the rest of us did, and although she was pleased with herself, she had banged her mouth when she crashed at the bottom, and the blood poured.

'I've had enough,' she said, when we picked her up and congratulated her. 'Why don't we fix Aristotle's hair?'

'I haven't seen the Headquarters yet,' Clio pointed out. 'And I've still got my money for the Fund. That old Puffer chased us off before I could put it in.'

We showed her the Humber. She complained that it smelt stuffy, so we took the Fund outside and counted it. I put in another ninepence and Rosie added a shilling. With Clio's fifteen bob it now stood at thirty-four shillings and threepence halfpenny.

'That means nearly half of it's mine. How much did the rest of you put in?' Clio asked.

'Oh, I dunno. It doesn't matter, does it?' Sid said, surprised.

She wriggled her shoulder and pouted. 'I just want to know. I'm a member of the Committee now, I ran down that horrible Wall. So I've a *right* to know, haven't I?'

To satisfy her, we worked it out. Rosie and I had put in more than Sid, and Algy had put in less than anyone, owing to the system of fines his parents operated; he lost a proportion of his pocket money whenever he got bad marks for a piece of homework or a low percentage in a school test. This week I had helped him with his homework on the way home and so he had done better than usual, but he had lost his school cap and his mother had kept his ten shillings towards the cost of a new one.

'That's only what Algy says, isn't it?' Clio said. 'How d'you know he's not spent it?'

Sid, Rosie and I were so stunned by this suggestion that we were temporarily winded: we stared at her in silence, our mouths hanging open. Algy looked miserable. Clio had the grace to seem ashamed: she coloured up a little and tossed her head. 'It just seems a bit funny to me,' she said crossly. 'I mean he's much richer than the rest of us, he's got a huge house and two cars.'

'His parents have,' Sid said. 'That's not the same thing.'

'I can see what she means, though,' Algy said. 'It doesn't seem fair.'

'Oh, don't be a nit,' I said, exasperated. 'It's not your fault. You can't help the parents you were born with.'

'I needn't have lost my school cap, though. We were just fooling around in the train and someone chucked it on to the line.' He looked ashamed and unhappy. 'I tell you what. I could sell my bike. It's got a hub dynamo and a speedometer.'

'Oh, don't talk stuff and nonsense,' Rosie cried, turning on him so suddenly that he took a step backwards for safety— Rosie is quick with her fists when she's roused. It comes of being Irish, Sid says, and being the eldest of her family. She has to keep the younger ones in order whenever her mother has another baby, which happens about once a year. But she didn't hit Algy this time, only raged at him. 'What d'you think your ruddy parents would say if you did? You'd have to say you'd lost the bike or something, and then you'd lose your pocket money for just about the next *ten years*. You want your head examined, Algernon Francis Beecham, you really do!'

Of course, it wasn't Algy she was angry with really. She wouldn't say anything to Clio in front of the rest of us, out of pride, but while Sid and I got Aristotle out of the Humber, she walked Clio off a little way. We could see Clio hanging her head and Rosie waving her arms about. Then, when Rosie came back, Clio went off on her own, wandering over the dump and kicking at the rubbish.

Rosie said, 'I told her to apologise to Algy, but I don't suppose she'll be able to get it out. She's not very good at saying she's sorry.'

'Who is?' Sid said. 'Though honestly Rosie, she *is* pretty awful.'

'No one likes her at school,' Rosie admitted. 'But her parents aren't here. Her father's a sergeant in the Army and he's stationed in Aden and she's staying with her Aunt. Her Aunt's not nasty to her or anything, and she gives her a lot of money to spend, but she's out a lot in the evenings. Clio hates being alone, she's frightened of the dark, and where her Aunt lives, over the shoe shop in the High Street, there aren't any neighbours. I think Clio has an awful time, really.'

Sid lifted an eyebrow at me and I grinned back. We understood now. Rosie likes people who have troubles. She collects lame ducks—well, not ducks exactly, but stray dogs, cats, budgerigars, anything she finds that needs looking after. There's always plenty of milk in her house because of all the babies, and Rosie's mother said she once counted twenty-seven cats lapping away from saucers at the back door. That was the time she made a rule that there were to be no more than five stray animals actually inside the house: after that, Rosie had to put the others in the garage or in sheds in the garden.

Algy was staring after Clio who glanced back once, and then, when she saw we were looking, ran a bit further away and sat down with her back to us, hugging her knees. I felt quite sorry for the awful girl. It's the hardest thing in the world to come back and face people when you've behaved badly to them.

'Go and fetch her, Rosie,' I said. 'Tell her we're going to finish Aristotle.'

Rosie gave me what my Gran would call an old-fashioned look. 'Better if you went, Fred. She thinks you don't like her.'

'She thinks right, then. But we can't get on with anything, with her glooming about the place.'

'I'll go,' Algy offered, but Rosie shook her head.

'Best to just leave her. She'll come when she's simmered down a bit.'

It was nice and hot in the sun, so we got Aristotle out of the Humber and sat by the river while Sid and I plaited strands of grey wool and Algy stitched them on, under Aristotle's tweed hat. Rosie added a few artistic touches: a scarlet handkerchief in his breast pocket, a pair of kid gloves and a smart, spotted bow tie she'd pinched from her father. When we were almost finished, Clio came back. Standing a little way off, she said, 'He ought to have a stick down his back, to make him sit straight.' She spoke in a very polite voice, like someone trying to think of something to say at a party.

'Have you got one?' Sid asked, not looking at her and speaking in an off-hand way as if she had been helping us all the time.

'Here,' she said, rather breathlessly, and produced a short pole from behind her back.

We said it was just the right length and it was clever of her to find it and she helped us to fix the pole under Aristotle's jacket. We sat him by the river. Unless you went very close, he looked like a man sitting quiet and dozing in the sun. 'Like someone fishing,' Algy said, which gave me a splendid idea.

The fishing was private in this stretch of river, and though old Puffer had turned a fairly blind eye to our activities on the site so far, it would have been a different matter if he'd once caught any of us with a rod and line, or even a jam jar. He'd caught four boys fishing in the summer, taken their names and had them hauled up before the magistrate. There was nothing in the weedy old river except a few perch and an occasional pike, so it was stupid of him to be so conscientious about it.

I propped Aristotle up against the notice which said, 'Private, Milton Reach Angling Society'. Rosie found a long stick and tucked it under his arm. 'By the time it's getting dark, it'll look just like a rod,' she said.

There wasn't long to wait. A bit before six o'clock, we piled into the Humber and waited. Clio got a giggling fit, putting her hand over her mouth and rolling her eyes round so we could see how big and blue they were, until Sid turned on her and said he'd jolly well push her out of the car and let old Puffer catch her, if she didn't shut up.

Algy was look-out, peering through the little window at the back of the car. That's usually his job because he doesn't get bored the way Sid and I do with waiting and watching. 'He's coming,' he whispered now, and we all dodged down and held our breath while Puffer trudged round the outskirts of the car cemetery towards the river. As he approached the Humber, his footsteps stopped. We lifted our heads cautiously. Old Puffer was about twenty yards away from Aristotle, standing stock still and staring.

He shouted, 'Hey. Hey you . . .' Naturally enough, Aristotle took no notice. 'This is private fishing, don't you know that?' Puffer went on. Still no reply from the trespasser. Old Puffer— he was half turned towards the Humber, so we had a good view of his face—looked thoroughly flummoxed. 'Can't you hear me, are you *deaf*?' he yelled.

Then, quite suddenly, his face changed. The puzzled look vanished and was replaced by a growing horror: even in the dimming light, we could see the colour drain out of his skin. Sid gave a stifled yelp of laughter and Clio nudged him in the ribs with a smug, reproachful look. 'He thinks it's a *dead man*,'

Sid choked, doubling up as if he had a stomach pain, and stuffing his sleeve into his mouth.

He was right. 'Oh, my God,' old Puffer cried in his wheezy old voice, and set off towards Aristotle in a stumbling run. He touched him on the shoulder and Aristotle fell sideways. Old Puffer began a sort of gargling scream, and then stopped short.

'God Almighty,' he shouted angrily. He glared round him, his expression changing horribly from fear to wild rage as he realised how he had been taken in. He began kicking poor Aristotle viciously in the side, until he rolled dangerously near the edge of the river. Then he bent and picked him up by one, limp arm.

'He'll throw him in,' Algy screamed, and hurtled out of the car. After a second's hesitation, we followed him and tore across the dump to the rescue. For a moment, we took old Puffer by surprise: he just stood there, staring at us in astonishment while we closed upon him. But we were too late. Though Algy managed to get hold of Aristotle's foot, Puffer had already recovered himself. He was an old man, but quite strong and anger made him stronger. He dragged the foot out of Algy's hands and with one, enormous heave, hurled poor Aristotle into the middle of the river. He sank with a splash, rose to the surface and began swirling away in the current.

Old Puffer turned to us. 'Now,' he said, '*now*. I'll give you what for . . .'

His face was white and twisted up as he lunged forward. He caught Algy by the arm and wrenched it cruelly behind his back. 'Stop that . . .' Rosie shouted and kicked old Puffer smartly in the calf. He whooped with pain and let Algy go.

'Run,' Sid cried, and then, as we ran, 'We've got to get him before he goes over the weir.'

There was no chance of catching Aristotle this side of the Wall because the bank is too steep and slippery there, and anyway old Puffer would have caught *us*. But the river runs in a culvert under Death Wall and into a tunnel under the railway, and beyond the tunnel the bank flattens out into a sort of landing ground, just before the weir.

So we made for Death Wall with old Puffer behind us, limping from the savage kick Rosie had given him and swearing terrible oaths. The things he was going to do to us when he caught us were very nasty indeed and I don't think any of us had ever gone up the slope so fast before. But in spite of our speed, by the time we had slithered down the embankment and reached the river, we were too late to rescue Aristotle. The current was running extra fast after the week's rain and half of him had already disappeared over the weir. The other half, his legless torso, had been caught on the posts and was slowly disintegrating as the foamy white water swirled round him.

Sheltering in the mouth of the tunnel so that old Puffer couldn't see us, even if he looked from the top of the wall, we watched Aristotle's end in silence.

When nothing was left of him that we could see, Rosie said sadly, 'That was the best guy I ever made. He had a lovely face, it took simply ages to make.'

'We can make another one,' Algy said.

Rosie sighed. 'I haven't the heart, somehow.'

Sid found a toffee in his pocket and handed it to her, without speaking. She sucked it slowly, staring at the water.

'There's another thing,' I said. 'We left the Fund behind.'

'Then you'd better go and fetch it, hadn't you?' Clio said.

'Who? Me?'

She nodded, looking smug. 'It was you thought of the joke with the guy, wasn't it? So you're the one who ought to risk going back, since it's all your fault.'

Sid said, 'That's rot. Honestly. I mean, none of us said it was a bad idea, did we? No one *objected* . . .'

Clio didn't answer him. She was looking at me with her mouth half open in a sly, pleased smile, the tip of her tongue just showing and gently stroking her upper lip.

'That's all right, Sid,' I said. 'I don't mind going back. I'm not scared of old Puffer.'

I went back straightaway, partly because I was maddened by that look on Clio's face, but chiefly because I reckoned that it was the safest moment to choose: old Puffer would be so certain he'd scared us off, that he wouldn't be expecting us to turn up again for a while.

As a theory this seemed convincing enough, but the moment I got over the Wall I began to doubt it: old Puffer might be so stupid that he hadn't worked it out, or so clever that he might guess *we* had. And, in the half-dark, and on my own, the site looked horribly sinister: I began to feel there were night watchmen lurking behind every scrubby bush, every looming, black shape. A rat scuttering over the dump made my mouth go dry; by the time I had got the Fund out of the Humber and raced back to the Wall, my legs were so shaky that my knees seemed to be bending backwards, and I had a struggle to climb up it.

Sid said, 'Well done, Fred,' and Rosie, 'Oh Fred, I'd have *died*,' which made me feel better because Rosie seldom praises anyone. Clio said nothing. It was almost dark by now and I couldn't see her face but I knew she was looking at me, so I said that it wasn't very difficult, really, and I was surprised they were making such a fuss about it.

Algy had to be home by seven on Saturdays, so we started back along the path. None of us felt much like talking, and Rosie was particularly gloomy. From time to time she sighed and said, 'Poor Aristotle . . .'

To cheer her up Sid and I began to discuss where we should build the bonfire on Firework Night. Rosie had the biggest garden of all, and the best-tempered mother, but we couldn't light a fire there, because it would frighten all the animals. Sid hadn't got a garden, nor had Clio. Mine was too tidy for bonfires, and as for Algy—well, it would have been easier to ask the Queen if we could light a small fire in the front of Buckingham Palace, than to ask Algy's mother.

'It's not going to be much fun anyway, now Aristotle's gone,' Rosie said drearily. 'There's no point in doing *anything*, if we haven't got a guy.'

'Well even if we haven't,' I said, 'we can light a pretty good fire in my Gran's back yard. I'll ask her if you like, she never grows anything there, she says there isn't enough sun, and it's full of good rubbish we can burn.'

CHAPTER FIVE

A FIREWORK PARTY AND
A CONFIDENCE TRICKSTER

JINNY SAYS I ought to say 'The Firework Party was the last carefree event of my youth.' I think this is rather an exaggerated way of putting it, although it would be true to say that after that evening at Gran's, nothing was ever quite the same again. The things we had to do were not only so dangerous, but so downright illegal as well, that they made racing the pram wheels and tormenting old Puffer seem very babyish stuff.

But this is to go on too fast. Before that—before things began to go wrong, that is—everything went suddenly and splendidly *right*. Not only did Gran say that we could have the bonfire in her garden and bake potatoes afterwards, but we collected an extra twenty-five shillings for fireworks. Or rather, Algy did.

Algy was given to brooding. If anyone said anything unkind to him, he worried over it. He had a very low opinion of himself, I suppose because his parents were always telling him how stupid he was, and so when Clio accused him of not putting a fair share into the Fund, he took it terribly to heart. 'I ought to have tried harder with my homework,' he said, over and over again. When Sid and I tried to argue with him and tell him it didn't matter, he just shook his head miserably. 'I ought to resign from the Committee, I'm not pulling my weight,' he said.

And he didn't say this to make us sorry for him: he really believed it.

Bonfire night was Sunday. On Saturday afternoon, I went to the Health Store for Gran, to buy some Nut Loaf for Mr Gribble's supper. The High Street was full of kids with guys in prams or boxes on wheels. None of the guys were as good as

Aristotle and I was feeling pretty bitter about that when I saw one that was not only better, but so marvellously life-like that I stopped in my tracks and stared.

This guy was sitting on the opposite pavement, leaning against a lamp post. He was tall and thin, with long legs sticking out in front and one hand laid across his chest and holding a notice that said *Spare a Penny For the Guy.* His head drooped sideways and he wore an old bowler hat and glasses. He looked just like Algy, I thought—and then I saw it *was* Algy. He wasn't moving, he sat there like a dead man. Even when I crossed the road and went up to him, he didn't twitch a muscle.

He was beginning to attract quite a lot of attention. A couple of girls were giggling and several women with shopping baskets had stopped to look. One of them said, 'What a marvellous idea. So *original.*' She had a silly voice and she wore a fur coat that made her look like a mangy Teddy Bear, but she wasn't as awful as she looked. While I watched, she opened her bag and took out half a crown and dropped it in an open tin by Algy's limp, right hand.

The tin was full of coins. Most of them were pennies, but there was a little silver, too. I whispered, in my best falsetto voice, 'My dear old chap, what would Thuggins say?' but except that one eyelid quivered a little, Algy gave no sign of having heard.

'He'll get cramp, poor lad,' a kind looking woman said. She gave him sixpence. Someone else said, 'I think it's plain cheek,' and another, 'Begging is against the law, it's disgraceful!' I thought I saw Algy wince a little at this. Then a man said, 'Don't be a spoil-sport, Edna, no harm in a bit of fun.' And there was another *chink* in the tin.

Quite a crowd was gathering, blocking the pavement. People on the outside seemed to think there had been a road accident. I heard one man say, 'Is the boy hurt, has someone sent for an ambulance?' A roar of laughter greeted this remark and the crowd parted a little to let the man through. When he saw his mistake, he began to laugh too, and dropped something in Algy's collection.

A policeman said, 'Move along now, keep the pavement clear.' He was watching Algy, but in a friendly way, as if he didn't want to stop the fun just yet. I knelt down, pretending to tie up my shoe lace. 'You're all right for a bit longer,' I said softly, and stood up again.

But it wasn't true. My heart turned over. *Algy's mother was walking along the opposite pavement.* She couldn't see Algy yet, there were too many people standing around, but in another minute she would draw level and she would be bound to glance across the road. Some mothers might laugh, but not Algy's mother.

'Algy,' I said. '*Algy.* It's your Mum.'

He gave me a shocked look, then jerked alive, arms and legs stiff like a puppet's. 'Legs gone to sleep,' he gasped. I heaved at him—though he's tall, he's quite light—and got him to his feet. We tottered across the pavement and almost fell against the policeman who was standing in a shop doorway, watching us.

Algy collapsed, leaning against the window, and moaned. The policeman stood over us, his big, blue bulk between us and the street. 'Rub his calves,' he advised. 'It'll get the blood back.' Then he frowned and added in a fierce voice, 'And don't let me catch you at this game again! Blocking the public highway!'

With Algy's twenty-five shillings added to the Fund, we were able to get a magnificent lot of fireworks. Rockets and Roman Candles and Atom Bombs and Catherine Wheels and Jumping Jacks and several packets of coloured sparklers especially for Clio. We built the bonfire with a lot of old wooden crates Gran had in her back yard. Then she called us in for tea.

She'd laid the round table before the fire with sandwiches and cakes and a big dish of hot crumpets, dripping with butter.

There was lemonade for us and besides Mr Gribble's place, Gran had put a mug and spoon and his jar of Hubbel's Fluid. 'He said he'd be back for tea,' she said. 'I can't think where he's got to.'

'I don't suppose he's very keen on fireworks, Gran,' I said.

She looked reproachful. 'Maybe not, but he likes to see other people enjoying themselves.' She gave a little sigh. 'He says it's the only happiness he finds in life now, the poor man.'

But he didn't come. We polished off the cake and the sandwiches and all the crumpets except two, which Gran put in the oven to keep warm for Mr Gribble. 'I expect he's been kept on some errand of mercy,' she said, shaking her head sadly. 'Looking after some poor soul who needs a helping hand.'

I said, 'If he enjoys making other people happy, I can't see why you're so sorry for him.'

'Because there's no gratitude in this old world,' Gran said, sounding suddenly like herself again, and not like an echo of Mr Gribble. She smiled at me. 'He wouldn't want us to wait for him, though. What about lighting the bonfire now?'

It was a splendid fire. It blazed and crackled and sent sparks shooting up into the air. Sid let off the first rocket and it soared up with a *whoosh*, banging three times before it let fall a shower of red and yellow stars. 'Oh *my*,' Gran said. 'Oh *my*.'

'Grown-ups don't usually like fireworks,' Clio said, in a superior voice and Gran gave her a funny look. 'I must be in my second childhood then,' she said, and gasped as a Catherine Wheel got going: flying sparks on the outside, yellow further in, and, right in the centre, a little circle of blue feathers.

We let off the rest of the fireworks. Clio, who had said she was scared of bangs, got wilder than anyone and rushed round the garden shouting, *bang, bang, bang, oh, please let me let off the next one, Sid . . .*

It was all over much too soon. We had kept the best rocket until the end, and it wouldn't light properly. Sid said, 'Last year's stock, I shouldn't wonder. That's my last match, too. Have you got another, Mrs B?'

'In the teapot, Fred,' she said. 'And bring the potatoes at the same time. The fire's low enough now.'

I went into the kitchen and got the potatoes out of the sack beside the sink. Then I went to the dresser and took the teapot down. There were the bits of string Gran kept there, folded into little skeins, and a half sheet of stamps and a box of matches. I took out the matches and put the lid back on the teapot and then something struck me. I took the lid off again, and looked. There was just the string and the stamps. Nothing else.

I went into the garden and gave Sid the matches. I said, 'Gran, did you put your money in the Post Office after all?'

The last rocket went up. I was watching it and thinking it was rather a cheat because it had cost twice as much as any of the others and wasn't any better, when Gran said, 'What do you mean?'

The light from the bonfire was flickering over her face and she looked thin and rather pale, '*What* did you say, Fred?' she repeated.

The last rocket star burst in the sky and went out. I said, 'I only asked, Gran.' I thought perhaps she was angry with me for interfering, so I added, 'I wasn't poking my nose in, or anything. I just saw the money wasn't there, so I thought you must have put it in the Post Office or in a bank.'

She turned and went into the house. I followed her and found her standing by the dresser, the teapot in her hand. 'It's gone,' she said.

'I know, I told you,' I began, and then I saw the expression on her face. 'D'you mean you didn't *know*?'

Gran sat down on the kitchen stool and nodded.

'Someone's *stolen* it?' I couldn't quite believe it and clearly Gran couldn't either. She just sat, staring into the teapot.

The others crowded in the doorway. 'What's the matter, Fred?' Sid asked.

'Someone's taken Gran's money. What she was keeping for a rainy day.'

'In a *teapot?*' Clio said, as if she had never heard of anyone doing such a thing.

'Oh, shut up,' Sid said. He went over to Gran and took the teapot away from her. 'Come and sit down, Mrs B,' he said, 'we'll get you a nice cup of tea. Put the kettle on, Algy.' And he helped her through into the sitting room, sat her down in her chair, and put some more coal on the fire.

Gran lay back with her eyes closed. She looked very old and small and we all stood round, looking at her.

'Perhaps she's fainted,' Rosie whispered. 'We ought to put her head down between her knees.'

Gran opened her eyes. 'Don't worry, I'll live.' She tried to smile at us and then said, pathetically, 'Has it really gone, Fred?'

I nodded. I couldn't speak.

'How much was it?' Algy asked.

'Forty-five pounds,' I said.

Sid gave a low whistle and covered up by poking energetically at the fire.

'Forty,' Gran said. She caught my eye. 'I had some unexpected expenses.' She gave a little cough as if something had embarrassed her. 'Well, that's that. It'll teach me a good lesson. Keeping all that money in the house!' Her voice was stronger now, almost cheerful, but her hands were clenched tight in her lap and the veins stood out on the backs.

Sid said, 'Who knew the money was there, Mrs B?'

'I did,' I said. I thought I caught a flicker on Clio's face and rounded on her. 'But I didn't take it, so there.'

'I didn't say you did.' Clio's lip trembled a little.

'Oh don't be mean, Fred,' Rosie said.

Sid frowned at us impatiently. 'Who else knew?' he asked.

Gran looked down at her hands and unclenched them, very slowly. Then she stared into the fire and a slow blush crept up her face.

'*Mr Gribble*,' I said.

She gave a long, trembling sigh. 'He told me he'd given his week's wages away to some poor woman he'd met. And I could see he needed a new pair of shoes. He'd only got one pair and they had newspaper in the soles. I gave him five pounds last night. I suppose he saw me take it out of the teapot.' She looked at me. 'I've been a fool, Fred. A stupid silly *old* fool.'

Sid turned and went up the stairs. I followed him. The bedroom looked as if no one had ever slept there: no clothes in the wardrobe or the chest of drawers, nothing on the tables, nothing under the bed. The only sign that Mr Gribble had ever been there, was a towel draped over the picture Sid and I had hung up the day he came. Sid stared at this. 'Gran told Mum that he didn't like the picture,' I explained. 'He said it was lewd, whatever that means.'

'Extra rude,' Sid said. 'But if he didn't fancy it, why didn't he just ask your Gran if he could take it down, for Heaven's sake?' He edged round the bed and tugged at the towel. There was nothing behind it except an empty frame: the picture itself had gone.

We clattered down the stairs. 'He's pinched the picture too,' I shouted. 'He's a thief.'

'*And* a confidence trickster,' Sid said. 'That's what they do. They go round telling people all sorts of stories and getting them to give them money for shoes and things. I expect he had lots of shoes, really. He just wore an old pair to make your Gran sorry for him.'

Algy made the tea and Gran was drinking it. She looked better now. 'Oh, I don't mind about the old picture,' she said. 'Except that Albert was fond of it . . . But to be taken in like that at my time of life!' She put the cup down in the saucer with a clash. Her hand was trembling and Algy took the cup from her and put it down on the table.

'When did he leave, Mrs B?' Sid asked.

'This morning, it must have been. I went out to do my

shopping and when I came back, he'd gone. I didn't go up to his room, he always kept it tidy and made his own bed. Didn't want to be too much trouble to me, he said. He was going to get a bit of lunch out because I'd be busy getting tea ready, and I told him to be sure and get those new shoes.' Gran leaned back in her chair and gave a low groan. 'He said I was a True Friend . . .'

'Of all the nasty creeping *snakes*,' Sid said. I'd never seen him so angry: his face was brick red and his blue eyes blazed. 'We've got to go straight to the police, Mrs B.'

'No,' Gran said. 'No . . .'

Her voice was low but firm. For a minute, we were all silent with astonishment. Then Rosie said, 'But they'll catch him, and then you'll get your money back.'

'And *he'll* go to prison,' Clio said. 'He *ought* to go to prison.'

Sid was staring at Gran. 'You don't mean you're sorry for him, Mrs B? You don't still believe all those things he said? About being a good man and helping other people?'

Gran shook her head. 'No. I know those were lies. But I don't want anyone to go to the police.' She looked at me. 'Fred, don't take this amiss. Your mother's been a good daughter to me, I'll not deny it. But you know what she'd say about this. I'd never hear the last of it. It's my own stupid fault and I'm a silly old woman who ought to have known better, but I don't want to hear her say it over and over again for the rest of my life. I'd rather lose forty pounds.'

I said uncomfortably, 'Mum wouldn't be like that, Gran. Not over something important, like this.'

She smiled at me. It was a real smile, not forced. 'Maybe you're right, but I don't want to risk it. Call it silly pride, if you like.'

'But Gran. . .' I was going to argue, but Sid kicked me on the ankle, and I stopped.

'There's one other thing,' he said. 'You said he'd given his week's wages away.'

'To some poor soul in trouble,' Gran said grimly.

'So he . . . I mean he didn't pay you for this week?'

Gran shook her head. Sid opened his mouth to say something, then changed his mind and shut it again. Gran looked at us all.

'Now,' she said, 'I want you to promise me something. I want you to forget about the whole thing.' None of us moved or spoke and she sighed a little. 'Look at it this way. I wouldn't have spent that forty pounds, I daresay, so I'm no worse off, really, now that it's gone. And I don't want a lot of old talk and chatter in the town, and people saying, *she's too old to look after herself, she's gone weak in the head, she ought to be put in a home!*'

'No one would say that,' I cried.

'Yes they would,' Rosie said. We all looked at her, surprised, and she went pink. 'I mean, people who didn't know your Gran *might* say it. I know, because there was a nice old lady lived in a bungalow down our street and she kept goats and chickens in the house and people said she was—well, like your Gran said, a bit weak in the head, and they sent for the Sanitary Inspector. And then they took her away and put her in a home. It wasn't fair, because she was quite all right really. I used to visit her sometimes to see the animals. She had an old rooster called Archibald after her husband. He used to perch on the end of her bed at night. And a goat called Harry . . .'

'Time *I* bring goats and chickens into my bedroom I'll be ready for my box,' Gran said tartly. Then she looked at Rosie and her face softened. 'But you're on the right track, my girl. Once you get old, you can't be too careful. You're no help to anyone and a nuisance to most—it's best to toe the line and be no more of a nuisance than you can help. So I want you to promise me you won't breathe a word to anyone. It's my forty pounds, after all.'

Though she laughed, we could tell she was serious about it.

Algy said, 'I'd feel the same if it was *my* money'd been stolen. I'd die rather than let my parents know.' Behind his glasses, his eyes went round with horror. 'I'd *kill* myself.'

'That's different, you're just a kid,' Sid said. 'They can do *anything* to you. . .'

'Kids and old people are in the same boat in that way,' Gran said. 'Have you ever thought of that?' She looked at us steadily, one by one. 'So do you promise me?'

We glanced at each other and nodded.

Gran said, 'Well, that's that then.' She leaned back and looked, all at once, very tired. So tired, that I was suddenly afraid she was going to die soon. My chest felt tight as if something was swelling up inside it. I wanted to put my arms round her and hold her tight, but I couldn't do that with the others looking on. I said, 'Is there anything we can do, Gran?'

'No, Fred. Just go home and forget all about it. Least said, soonest mended.' She smiled at us all. 'And thank you for a lovely Firework Party,' she said.

At the end of the street, we stopped to talk.

'It's worse than just losing the money,' Sid said. 'I bet he didn't pay her a penny. And she had to feed him and all.'

'She owes at the Health Store,' I said. 'I went shopping for her Saturday, and she said to put it on the bill.'

'I wish we hadn't spent all that on fireworks, just going up in *smoke*,' Algy said miserably.

Clio said. 'Couldn't we get up another Fund? I mean, we couldn't save forty pounds, not for years, but we could save a bit . . .'

'Gran wouldn't take it if we did.'

'We could send it through the post. Anonymously. Just say *From a well-wisher* that sort of thing,' Clio looked at me and swallowed. 'And I didn't think you'd pinched your Gran's money, so *there*.'

This frontal attack took me by surprise. 'Well, you know what you are', I said, rather weakly.

'*What* am I?' Her face was stoney.

'Well . . .' I began, but Sid turned on me.

'Oh, give over, Fred. We'll never do anything if you keep on quarrelling with Clio, haven't you any sense?'

'We can't do anything anyway,' I grumbled. 'We promised Gran.'

'Only that we wouldn't tell anyone, that's all. We never said we wouldn't *do* anything. And there are two things we can do. First, we can collect some money, as Clio said. Algy—since you're so good at that sort of thing, you'd better arrange it.'

Algy beamed. Even his glasses seemed to sparkle with pleasure.

'It's half-term Monday and Tuesday,' Sid said, 'so you've got two full days to get cracking. Rosie—you'd better help him. And Clio. Fred and I are going to be busy.'

'Doing what?'

Sid looked astonished. 'Why, finding Mr Gribble, of course.'

'Don't be dead daft. He'll have gone off, won't he? D'you think he'll just turn up at Puttock's shop, Monday? He'll have disappeared from the scene of the crime—why, he might be in Scotland by *now!*'

'I doubt that,' Sid said. 'I don't suppose Puttock'll know where he is, but he might have some clue.'

Clio said, 'But you can't tell Mr Puttock why you want him, can you? I mean, we promised.'

'What sort of clue, anyway?' Rosie said. 'I mean thieves don't usually leave forwarding addresses when they run away, do they?'

Sid looked harassed. 'I didn't say it was going to be easy, did I?'

'I should think it was pretty impossible,' I said.

'We're only kids. It's not as if we were police, or something,' Rosie said.

'I mean, where'd you *start*?' Algy said.

Sid stared round the circle. His expression said that he despised us all. 'I don't know yet,' he said. 'All I know is, you're just about the dreariest, feeblest lot of half-wit goons I ever met in my whole life. If you don't want to find Mr Gribble just say so—don't bother to argue, just *say* so and I'll know exactly where I am. But whatever you say, I know one thing. Even if I have to do it on my own, I'm going to find him and get that money back. If it's the last thing I do.'

CHAPTER SIX

ADVICE FROM UNCLE WILLIAM

'WELL, WHAT D'YOU want?'

The notice on the door of the Antique Shop said, 'Walk In Any Time. No Obligation to Buy.' Mr Puttock himself, who had been taking a snooze in a deep armchair at the back of the shop, did not seem so welcoming. He looked at us blearily and repeated, 'Come on now, what do you want?'

He was a fat man. The fat hung round his jaw in folds, pulling down the lower rim of his eyes as if his cheeks were too heavy for his face.

Sid nudged me. 'I want to see Mr Gribble,' I said politely. 'I've got a message for him.'

'Want to see Gribble, eh?' Mr Puttock laughed—*hur, hur.* Hollow and deep like the sound in a tunnel. 'Well, it's more than I do.'

I tried to look surprised. 'Isn't he working here, then?'

'Was. Got rid of him. Got on my nerves.'

'Oh, what a dreadful *nuisance*,' I said. I thought my voice sounded high and silly and was afraid Mr Puttock would know I was acting. 'Do you know where he is now?'

'No. Nor want to. Talk, talk, talk, boom, boom, boom— it made me tired. Put the customers off, too.'

'Oh.' I hesitated. 'It's a pity because we wanted to see him most particularly.'

'What for?' He peered at me closely with his droopy, blood-hound eyes. 'You're Mrs Blackadder's grandson, aren't you? What's the matter? Gribble skipped without paying the rent?'

Sid thumped me in the back. 'Say he left something behind,' he hissed in my ear.

'Oh, no.' I laughed loudly. 'It's just that he left a few things behind, by mistake. Gran was worried in case he needed them.'

'So she sent you round after him? Didn't he tell her he'd left the shop, then?'

Mr Puttock was looking at me curiously. I was afraid he knew I was lying and I looked him straight in the eye to show that I wasn't.

'I don't know,' I said. It seemed the safest answer.

'Oh well, maybe she didn't.' He frowned. 'Seems a bit queer, but then he's a queer sort of chap.' He looked at me again and his expression was suddenly sharp. 'You're sure there's no trouble? He's not upset your grandmother in any way?'

'Oh, of course not.' I made my eyes wide and surprised.

'That's a good thing, then.' Mr Puttock eased himself up out of his chair with a sigh that made his dewlaps tremble. 'Fine woman, your grandmother, I wouldn't want her upset. Tell her not to worry over Gribble's things, he'll be back if he wants them. And tell her if she's got any more pictures, I'll be pleased to take a look at them.'

'P-pictures?' I stammered.

'Like that one.' Mr Puttock's white hand waved towards the wall of the shop and even before I looked, I knew what I should see hanging there. Gran's picture of the fat lady on the sofa.

Of course, I thought, *I should have guessed*. 'I didn't know Gran was going to sell that,' I said.

Mr Puttock laughed. *Hur, hur*. 'I must say I was a bit surprised myself when Gribble brought it in. Mind you, I knew she had some good stuff, but I didn't think she was keen to get rid of it. Pity it wasn't framed, though. I found one for it, but it's a bit ordinary. Your grandfather was the one to go to for framing, young man, did you know that?'

Sid muttered, 'Ask him what he paid for it.' Mr Puttock glanced at him in a puzzled way and Sid hung his head and shuffled his feet.

'Is the picture worth a lot?' I asked.

'Things are worth what they'll fetch. Now that's quite a nice little picture, but not everyone's taste, you know. Too ornate. I may make a profit on it or I may not. It's all a gamble in this trade.' His eyes went past us to the door. The bell jangled as a man and a woman came in. 'Give my regards to your grand-mother,' he said, and lumbered forward to meet them.

'What cheek,' Sid said. 'What frightful cheek. Fancy pinching it and selling it to old Puttock!'

'Who does it belong to now? After all, Puttock's paid for it.'

'I dunno,' Sid said. 'I should think it's your Gran's, really. In *law*, I mean. It's stolen property, you can't legally sell stolen property, can you?'

I didn't know the answer to this, but it didn't seem very important. There was nothing we could do about it except tell Puttock the truth and we had promised Gran not to do that.

'We'll see about the picture after we've got the money back,' Sid said. 'And we can't get the money till we find Mr Gribble so we better get on with it. I vote we go to the station. He may not have caught a train but if he did, the station's not very busy, Saturdays, so someone might remember.'

It seemed a bit like looking for a needle in a haystack to me. 'Well, it's your turn to ask,' I said.

Sid shook his head. 'I can't. I don't know why, my tongue ties up in knots.'

So when we got to the station, I went up to the booking office and Sid hung behind. A train was just pulling out and the office was still open. A man with ginger hair stood there. He had a bad-tempered look and my heart sank. I said we were trying to find out if someone we knew had caught a train on Saturday. 'He had a long nose,' I said, 'and a sad face and he was wearing a raincoat that was much too big for him.' The book-ing clerk looked baffled and angry at first, and then just plain angry. 'What d'you think this is, a detective agency?' he said, and slammed the window shut.

'What d'you want son?' someone said behind me. It was a tall Jamaican porter, and he was smiling.

'Just a man,' I said. 'A sad looking man in a raincoat. I expect he'd be carrying a suitcase and he might have caught a train sometime on Saturday.'

The Jamaican's smile broadened. 'Not very easy son. A lot of men wear raincoats and a lot of them are sad. If he was a happy looking man now, you'd have more chance of finding him. Certainly in *this* country.' He laughed as if this was an enormous joke. 'What d'you want him for?'

Sid and I glanced at each other. We had thought of several things to say if we were asked this question. I came out with what I thought was the best one. 'It's my uncle,' I said. 'He's gone stark mad and stolen some secret drawings from the aircraft factory to sell to a Foreign Power. We can't go to the police because they'll put him in prison for a traitor, so we've got to find him before the papers are missed from the factory. He's not really a wicked spy, you see, just mad, and my aunt's terribly worried.'

He said slowly, 'I think I've seen him, son. A miserable looking fellow with a kind of mad glitter in his eye? He caught a train Saturday night, and I can tell you where. He bought a one way ticket to Moscow.'

He spoke so solemnly that I almost believed him. Then his face seemed to split open with laughter. He slapped his thigh and laughed and laughed. The noise echoed from the station roof. A train came in and he wiped his eyes and went to stand by the barrier. 'Kids,' he said, 'goddam kids,' and chuckled to himself while the people came off the train and gave him their tickets and looked at him queerly, as if wondering what he was so cheerful about.

'I can't see what was so funny,' I said, annoyed. 'After all, it might have been true.'

'Too far-fetched,' Sid said. 'It would have been better if you'd said it was my father who'd run away from home and my mother was crying. Anyway, I don't suppose he'd know. I watched him taking those tickets. He didn't look at people's faces just at their hands.'

'So it's no good.' I felt, suddenly, very let down.

'Well, *that* isn't. Oh—don't pull that face, you give up too easy. The next thing to do is to get hold of my uncle. Uncle William.'

'What can he do?'

'Well. You know he's on Safe Transit? Drives round in an armoured car with the money from banks, that sort of thing? He's got lots of friends in the police and . . .'

'We can't tell the police,' I said firmly.

'If you'd kindly let me *finish*. He can ask, can't he? Not say about your Gran, just ask if they know of someone like Gribble going round pinching money. The police have lists of people, descriptions, that sort of thing. All he's got to ask is if they know of someone like him who's a confidence trickster. Him being a vegetarian sort of stands out, doesn't it? So they might know something, we might get a *clue*.'

'All right,' I said, not because I believed him but because I couldn't think of anything else to do.

'We'll go round tea time,' Sid said. 'He's off duty early on Mondays.'

On the way to Sid's uncle, we met Algy and the others. Algy was pushing a pram and looking rather self-conscious. There was a baby inside, lying on its back and blowing bubbles. 'That's George,' Rosie said. 'Mum said she didn't mind what I did today but I'd got to take him with me. He's cutting a tooth and fretting but he's better when he's on the move.'

Clio said excitedly, We're collecting jumble in the pram. We've got a lot of things already and we're going to have a sale at the end of the week.'

'You won't get much for this,' Sid said, poking about at the baby's feet. They'd got a few old cups, a saucepan with a hole in it that someone had mended with plaster, three or four hats and something that looked like a dead cat. 'That's a real fur cape,' Rosie said proudly.

I held it up. It had a funny smell and lot of holes.

'Moth,' Rosie said. 'But I thought I'd darn it over with brown wool. I don't know what sort of fur it is.'

'Yak,' Sid said. 'Tibetan yak, I should think. And one that died about a million years ago. I suppose it might fetch something.' But he sounded doubtful.

'You have to take a lot of awful things to get one good thing,' Algy said. 'We went to one house and the man said we could have their grand piano if we could take it away. Of course we can't do that, but I thought if we asked while we're collecting if anyone wanted one, someone might. Then *they'd* have to collect it, and we'd get a commission.'

I stared at him. 'What d'you say you're collecting *for*?'

'Old people.' Algy grinned. 'Well, it's true in a way, isn't it?' He looked at his watch. 'Come on, girls. We've got to do Acacia Road before tea.'

We watched them disappear down the street. I felt rather envious. Collecting jumble was a great deal easier than trying to find Mr Gribble.

When we rang Uncle William's front door, a dog began baying —an awful, deep-throated bark that made my blood run cold. 'It's all right, that's Jake, he wouldn't hurt a fly,' Sid said.

We saw a gigantic shadow on the other side of the glass of the door. Someone said, 'Down Jake, down sir.' Then, 'Who is it?'

'Only me, Uncle William.'

'Half a mo' then.'

There was the rattle of chains and the sound of bolts being drawn back.

'He's scared of burglars,' Sid whispered.

My mouth dropped open. 'Scared of *burglars*? Someone who drives armoured cars?'

'Perhaps that's why,' Sid said.

But when the door opened it seemed absurd that Sid's uncle should be scared of anything. He was the biggest man I had ever seen, not fat like Mr Puttock, but huge-framed with a chest like a gorilla.

'Sorry to keep you waiting,' he said. 'You can't be too careful nowadays.'

He led the way down a tiny hall to a tiny sitting-room. The dog Jake stood on the hearth, every hair on his thick back erect and bristling. He was unlike any dog I had ever seen before.

Uncle William saw me looking at him. 'Cross between an Alsatian and a mastiff,' he said. 'But harmless as a kitten.'

'It's all right, Jake,' Sid said. 'This is my friend. Go on, stroke him, Fred.'

I took a step forward and stopped. I would as soon have stroked a tiger.

'You'll get used to him,' Uncle William said. 'Like to see a trick? Give me your hanky.'

I gave him my handkerchief, which was rather grubby. Sid sat down and took off a shoe. Uncle William added one of his own slippers and put the things in the middle of the floor. 'Watch now,' he said.

Jake went up to the things and sniffed. 'Go on Jake, back to their owners,' Uncle William said.

Jake picked out my hanky, brought it over to me, dropped Sid's shoe at his feet and laid Uncle William's slipper in his lap. Then he wagged his tail expectantly. Uncle William laughed—it was like a mountain laughing—and gave him a chocolate out of a box on the table. He passed the box on to Sid and me and then sat down and looked at us.

'What's up, Sid?' he asked, and I was surprised for a minute because we had given no hint that anything was wrong. Then I decided that Sid's uncle must be like my Gran. She always knows when something is bothering me.

'Bit of trouble,' Sid said.

'Get it off your chest, then. What about some cocoa first? It's on the hob.'

And in a minute, we were sitting down with steaming mugs in our hands.

'It's in confidence,' Sid said. 'Strictest confidence. Can I tell him, Fred?'

It was the first time he had suggested we might tell Uncle William the truth. I suppose if he had done it before, I would have said no. But when I looked at Uncle William, I couldn't see any harm in it: he was the sort of person you trust at once.

I nodded, and Sid began. Uncle William listened. He didn't interrupt the way most grown-ups would have done, just nodded from time to time, and when Sid had finished he didn't answer for a little while, just stared into the fire.

At last, he said, 'Finding someone's one thing. What do you do when you have?'

'We don't know yet,' Sid said. 'I think he might be so scared when he saw us—well Fred, anyway, because he knows who he is—that he'll just hand over the money. After all, *he* doesn't know we won't go to the police, so we could sort of threaten him . . .'

Uncle William winced. 'Dangerous business, threatening people.'

'Maybe,' Sid said. 'But the first thing is to find him. Then we can work out what we'll do.'

'I don't suppose he's gone far,' Uncle William said. 'Small criminals don't. Not that what he's done is small, exactly, but the sort of man who'd take forty pounds from an old woman is small in his *mind*. Chances are, he'll stay in the district—not in the next street, mind, but somewhere not too far away. Won't have the imagination to do anything else, you know, and even if he had, he mightn't do anything different. London suburbs are very anonymous places. People come and go and no one takes much notice. No one asks questions about strangers the way they do in a small country town. My guess is that he'll just have moved into another suburb this side of London. Not Milton itself but Milton South or Cranbrook or Thurston Park. That doesn't mean he'll be easy to find. But if you do, you'll watch your step, won't you, Sid?'

Sid nodded. When his uncle got up to pour out more cocoa, he winked at me.

Uncle William said, 'Sort of place you want to watch are cafés, cinemas, that sort of thing. Parks, on a fine day. A man like that will often sit on a park bench and watch people. Probably won't take a job till the money runs out, you see, he'd rather try to pick up someone else he can live on. Parks are a good place for that. You meet lots of old ladies, exercising dogs ...'

'But that'll take *years*,' I said. 'We've got to go back to school on Wednesday.'

Uncle William looked thoughtful. 'I said it wouldn't be easy, didn't I? If you like, I'll have a word with my friend Sergeant Andrews— oh, just casual, like. I'll say I've heard of this bloke, he tried to touch a friend of mine and *she* got the idea it had happened before. I'll ask him if knows of anyone like this man, operating this side of London.'

'It seems so *daft*,' I said. 'Gran not going to the police. I mean it seemed all right when she said it first, but now it just sounds silly.'

'People are funny,' Uncle William said. 'Though your Gran sounds perfectly sensible to me. All that would happen if she went to the police is that there'd be a lot of fuss and talk, and she might not be any better off in the end. Even if they caught him, he might have spent the money. You can't get blood out of a stone.'

'So you think we're wasting our time?'

'Well, since you ask me, yes.' I pulled a face, and he went on hastily, 'But that doesn't mean there's no point in trying. Even if it's only to satisfy yourself, like.'

'We're going to get the money back,' Sid said. And there

was a look of such absolute faith on his face that neither of us said any more.

Faith might move mountains, as the saying goes, but it doesn't find thieves. We did what Uncle William said. We stopped the others collecting jumble and we spent Tuesday searching the neighbourhood. We looked in every café, every park, first in one suburb, then in the next. Once, I thought I saw him on a bus. I dropped my bike, jumped on at the lights, and then found it was a much older, fatter man, who had no real resemblance to Mr Gribble at all. I told the conductor that I had made a mistake and got on the wrong bus, but he didn't believe me and I had to spend my last fourpence on a one-stage fare.

Even Sid was cast down. He'd been to see his uncle at lunch-time and Uncle William had said the police knew nothing about Mr Gribble. They had several small-time criminals on their books, but no one quite like him.

Rosie said, on Tuesday evening. 'We'd have done much better just to go on collecting jumble. And we've got to go back to school tomorrow ...'

The next two days passed in an atmosphere of gloom. By Thursday night, I had decided that Uncle William was almost certainly wrong about Gribble being in the neighbourhood and that he had probably only suggested he might be, to keep us occupied and out of trouble. I remembered how convincing he had sounded, as if he really understood how someone like Mr Gribble would behave, and it suddenly seemed to me that it had been just grown-up cleverness on his part, giving us something to do that couldn't do any harm. And then suggesting, at the end, that even if we did find Mr Gribble, Gran would be unlikely to get her money back, so that we would have an excuse to abandon the chase when we got bored ... I was angry for a little while, because I felt he had tricked us, and then I began to wonder if perhaps, after all, he was right. Perhaps we were wasting our time ...

On Friday morning, Sid was late for school. He came in during the first lesson. Friday is the worst day to be late because old Thuggins takes us for algebra after Assembly, and he is a stickler for punctuality.

'Punctuality is the politeness of princes,' he said in his pompous voice—so much like Mr Gribble's that it was uncanny—'perhaps you will do me a favour, Sidney, and write that out one hundred times? And *not*, if you please, in my lesson.'

'Yes sir. I mean, no, sir,'—Sid said. He turned to come to his desk and his eyes were sparkling and he looked thoroughly cock-a-hoop, as if Old Thuggins had given him a present instead of a hundred lines.

He sat down next to me. His lips were moving silently and he looked as if he were going to burst. The moment our headmaster turned to write a formula on the blackboard, he leaned towards me and whispered, 'I've seen him, Fred, I've *seen him*.'

Old Thuggins has eyes in the back of his head. Without turning round, he said, 'You can make it two hundred times, while you are about it.'

CHAPTER SEVEN

TO CATCH A THIEF

'I saw him at the window,' Sid said.

The moment the bell rang for break, we had rushed into the playground, got hold of Algy, and gone into a huddle at the back of the lavatories while Sid told his story.

He had been on his paper round which took him to Thurston Park, on the far side of the big main road that ran from Milton all the way into London. It wasn't a proper place like Milton which had once been a town on its own before London grew and joined on to it and then spread beyond. (London was like a greedy sponge, Dad said once, sopping up towns like water.) Thurston Park had a few shops but no cinema or railway station. It was mostly road after road of little houses, built in pairs and all looking exactly alike with red roofs and tiny gardens. There was just one road that was different: a long road of much older, bigger houses, all rather run-down now and turned into flats or let out in rooms. The house where Sid swore he had seen Mr Gribble was one of these. It was called Lilac Lodge.

'Though there aren't any lilacs that I've seen,' Sid said. 'Just a few dusty laurels and the garden's a mess. Smells of cats and mouldy rubbish. I leave six papers there every day and eight on Sundays, but I never see a soul, just dump the papers in the porch with the empty milk bottles. Well, I'd done that, then I thought my tyre felt spongy so I stopped in the drive to pump it up but of course it wouldn't—it was a fast puncture, that's why I was late. And when I stood up, cursing a bit, he was standing at the window watching me. He dodged back as soon as he saw I'd seen him . . .'

'Why?' Algy asked.

'What d'you mean, *why*?'

Algy's face creased up anxiously the way it always did when he was asked to explain something. 'I—I mean it's not as if you were Fred.'

'What's my not being Fred got to do with it?'

'W-well. Just that Gribble knows Fred. But he doesn't know you, so why should he bother to hide?'

'He does know me. He's seen me with Fred.'

'Only that first day he came to Gran's' I said. 'And he didn't really *see* you, not to remember. Grown-ups don't.'

'Oh, well. Guilty conscience, I expect,' Sid said. 'It's not important, anyway.'

Algy looked crestfallen, so I said, 'You can't be sure, Sid. I mean, it might be important, it might be a clue.' I couldn't think what sort of clue. I went on, 'Anyway, are you sure it was him? After all, you thought you saw him in that café.'

Sid nodded. 'I know. And I did see him, too!'

'That's what I meant. You thought it was him then and it couldn't have been, not Mr Gribble eating *meat*. So you might have thought wrong this time, too.'

'I didn't.' Sid's face went closed and obstinate. He hates being contradicted.

Algy said quickly, 'Well, there's a way to find out, isn't there? We can go and watch the house and wait and see if Fred recognizes him too.'

Which was what we did. Algy said he couldn't come at first, but I thought of a plan: while Sid went to fetch Rosie and Clio—we had decided this was a job for the whole Committee—I rang up Algy's mother. I put on my most polite voice. 'This is Fred McAlpine speaking. Algy's going to be late home, I'm afraid. He's been kept behind after school.'

'What's he done wrong?' she said at once.

I winked at Algy who was standing in the telephone box beside me looking worried. 'Nothing, Mrs Beecham. Algy never gets into trouble.' My voice sounded so smarmy-polite that I had difficulty stopping myself laughing. 'It's just that he couldn't do some algebra today and the maths master said if he could stay behind after school he'd help him with it. Algy thought it was a good chance and he ought to take it, but he didn't want you to worry so he asked me to ring up.'

'Oh,' she said. 'Oh, I see.' She sounded as if she were disappointed because there was nothing she could be angry about. Then she thought of something. 'I must say I'm glad he's taking his work seriously at last. It's about time. All he seems to have thought of up to now is getting out of the house and playing with other boys whose parents seem to let them roam the streets till all hours. Sometimes I wish we'd sent him to a nice private school.'

I said soothingly, 'I know what you mean, Mrs Beecham. My mother says the same, some parents just aren't *responsible*.' I wondered if this was going too far: even Algy's mother might realise this was an unlikely thing for a boy to say. I added hastily, 'But the education at Milton High is very good, even if some of the boys are a bit rough.'

'That's what my husband says.' Her voice sounded more amiable now. 'And at least he's made *one* friend with nice manners. Thank you for ringing up, Frederick.'

'Not at all, Mrs Beecham.'

I put the receiver down and doubled up. I had a pain in my stomach from not laughing. Now I laughed until the tears came into my eyes.

Algy was looking nervous. 'Suppose she finds out, Fred? Suppose she writes to him and says thank you for helping me with my algebra?'

'We'll cross that bridge when we come to it,' I said. 'There's no time to worry over it now.'

We got on our bikes and went like the wind. We got to Thurston Park in record time and found the road quite easily. It was a long, twisty road with a lot of trees: most of the leaves were down and rustling on the pavements. The road was very quiet and most of the houses were hidden behind the trees. We went up and down several times before we found Lilac Lodge. There was a wooden sign but it had fallen down in the bushes beside the gate.

Just as we found it, Sid appeared. He had Clio perched on his crossbar. She was red in the face and squeaking with fright as he took her over the potholes in the road. Rosie came behind him, pedalling furiously on a bike that was much too small for her.

'Pouf—I'm *exhausted*,' she panted as she came up to us. 'My bike chain's broken, so I had to borrow my sister's. She'll be mad when she finds out. Have you seen him yet?'

'Have a heart, we've only just got here,' I said. 'We'd better not leave all our bikes together. It looks suspicious.'

We dumped our bikes at intervals up and down the road and went in through the gate of Lilac Lodge. The drive twisted and turned; it was so overgrown that there were places where the laurel bushes met over our heads. It was getting dark.

In front of the house, there was a circular lawn—a patch of mud, really, with a few, straggly bits of grey grass growing in it. The house was big and looming with a rickety glass porch that had panes missing. It had a dreary, derelict air. We found a place to hide among the laurels at the side of the lawn where there was plenty of room for us all and the branches grew overhead like a tent. As Sid had said, the whole place smelt of cats. Dead cats. Clio pulled a face and held her nose.

We settled down as comfortably as we could. The ground was soft, but damp and cold. Time seemed to pass very slowly. 'I wish he'd hurry up,' Algy whispered. 'I daren't be later than half past six.'

'It's only about quarter past five,' Sid whispered back. 'You got to be *patient*.'

'My leg's getting cramp,' Clio complained.

'Ssh. Someone's coming,' Rosie said.

The front door banged. We froze like statues. Someone's

feet crunched on the gravel in front of the porch, then there was a whirr and a flicker as he wheeled a bike out and the dynamo light came on.

We knelt on the soggy ground and peered through the gaps in the laurel branches. A man coughed in a wheezy way, and we recognised him. It wasn't Mr Gribble. It was old Puffer. He scooted a little way, then, as he passed us, cocked his leg over the bike and rode on.

'I expect he's going on duty,' Sid said. 'I didn't know he lived here, but it's the sort of crumby place he *might*. There's a notice in the window that says lodgings for single men, and I should think it's awfully cheap.'

Clio giggled nervously,' I hope he doesn't go poking round in the Cemetery.'

Rosie explained. 'We put the jumble in the car. We got a lot on Monday, after we saw you, and I took it home but Mum was in a bad mood because she had a headache and she said we had enough rubbish of our own. So we took it down and dumped it all in the Humber. It's a lot of old dresses and hats, mostly, so I shouldn't think old Puffer'd be very interested, even if he found it.'

'Where are you going to have the Sale?' Sid wanted to know.

'In my garage,' Rosie said. 'Mum won't mind that, she'll be in a better temper by Sunday. I thought we'd put up notices on the gate, and Algy's going to have a raffle.'

'Sixpence a ticket, First Prize a grand piano,' Algy said. 'We couldn't find anyone who wanted one, so it seemed a good thing for a raffle. And whoever wins, we just tell them they've only got to collect it.'

Sid said, 'Ssh—you're making too much *noise*.'

It was cold. A wind had got up and leaves blew over the ground with a papery noise. No one else came in or out of Lilac Lodge. I kept looking at my watch which had a luminous dial and I began to think it must have stopped but it hadn't: when I put it to my ear, it was still ticking.

After a little, Sid said softly. 'The light's come on in his room. That one—on the first floor, to the right of the porch.'

I crawled over to look. The curtains were not quite drawn and we could see the light, but no one inside the room. I said, 'If he's settled down for the evening, he won't come out again. He never went out after tea at my Gran's.'

'Maybe he's changed his habits,' Sid said.

Rosie whispered. 'Even if he does come out, what are we going to do?'

'If we all rushed at him together, we might overpower him,' Clio said. 'We could kick him in the stomach and tie him up.' She sounded as if she would enjoy that.

Sid shook his head. 'That 'ud be plain daft. He won't have the money on him, if he's got any sense. No—what we've got to do first is to make sure it's really *him*. Then we can make a proper plan. We don't want him to see us even, till we've got our plan good and ready.'

'What plan?' Clio asked.

'I haven't worked it out yet,' Sid said, rather shortly.

Algy said, 'I tell you what. If Sid thinks he won't have the money on him, then he'll have put it somewhere in his room, won't he? Can't we watch the house and wait till he goes out and then go and take it, when he's not there?'

'You mean *steal* it?' Rosie breathed.

'It wouldn't be stealing. I mean it doesn't belong to him.'

'That doesn't make any difference,' Sid said. 'Don't be a fool, Algy. It would still be stealing.'

'I don't see it.'

'Neither do I,' I said. 'I mean, it's my Gran's money, not his. He pinched it. We'd only be getting it back.'

'It isn't like that, though,' Rosie said. 'There was a man down our street lent his lawn mower to the man next door, and then they had a row over something and the man wouldn't give it back. So the first man—the one the mower belonged to—just went next door and took it, and the other man called the police and had him up for stealing and trespass and all sorts of things. Even though it was the man's own lawn mower . . .'

'I think that's stupid,' Clio said.'

'Maybe it's stupid,' Sid said. 'But it's the *law*.'

'Then it's a potty old law,' Clio said. 'And I don't see what it's got to do with *us*.'

'What do you mean? The law's to do with everybody.'

Clio tossed her head. 'I know *that*. All I mean is, Mr Gribble wouldn't dare *do* anything, if we did steal the money back. He's different from Rosie's man with the lawn mower—he'd just borrowed it, see, so he didn't mind sending for the police. But Mr Gribble wouldn't send for the police, would he, because he's a thief himself? We'd be quite safe.'

There seemed some sense in this. I said so and Sid heaved a deep sigh and said it was just like me to be taken in by such a foolish argument. 'We were talking about the law, *she* was just talking about not getting caught! Typical female logic,' Sid said with a snort.

'Not getting caught seems quite important,' I said in my most sarcastic voice, and Sid groaned aloud.

'So is the *law*,' he said.

'Do stop quarrelling,' Algy whispered. 'Someone's coming.'

He was right. A man's voice said, 'Come on now, out of there,' and a torch shone through the laurels, right into my face.

We crawled out slowly. It was a tall man with glasses. 'What d'you think you're doing, this is private property, you know?' he said.

None of us said anything for a minute. Then Clio spoke. 'I'm sorry. We were just playing.'

The man shone his torch on her face for a minute. Her yellow hair glinted in the light and her eyes looked very big and innocent. He said, in a gentler voice, 'Well, you shouldn't be playing here, should you? Run along, and play in your own gardens in future.'

We walked down the drive, feeling unutterably foolish. When we got into the street, Sid spoke for us all. 'Fat lot of good *we* are! Can't even keep quiet for half an hour.'

We collected our bikes and wheeled them a little way down the road. We didn't look at each other. At last, Algy said, 'What are we going to do tomorrow?'

'Split up,' Sid said. 'We'll watch the house, but we'd better do it two at a time. There were too many of us tonight, that was the trouble. We shouldn't have had so many people, crashing around like a lot of elephants in the undergrowth.'

'You made as much noise as the rest of us,' Algy said—rather sharply, for him.

'*One* at a time might be better,' I said. 'One person can't quarrel with *himself.*'

Sid chose to ignore the bitterness in my voice. 'You've got to have two, in case something happens. Then one can stay and watch or follow Gribble if he leaves the house and the other can go for reinforcements when necessary. I reckon I should start off tomorrow, soon as I've finished my paper round. That's about eight o'clock, he won't go out before that. Rosie better come with me.'

'Why not *me*?' I asked indignantly.

Sid smiled patiently. 'Because you and me are the only ones who's *seen* Gribble. So one of us has got to be on the watch all the time till the others have seen him too. If he hasn't gone out by eleven o'clock, say, you can come and relieve Rosie and me and bring one of the others with you. Till then you'd better stay at home so that one of us can telephone if he *does* go out.'

'All right. But what are we going to do *then?*'

Sid looked faintly wary. 'Follow him,' he said, after a short pause. 'Watch where he goes, what he does. Then we'll get a better idea what to do.'

There was a silence.

Clio said, 'If you ask me, it's all a waste of time. Just talk. You're not really going to do anything, are you?'

No one answered. Sid bent over his bike, pretending to examine the chain.

'No one did ask you,' I said, but I felt, suddenly, too depressed to go on. Clio was right. Though Sid had suggested plans for tomorrow, it was only as if for a sort of game. The fact was that apart from watching the house and following Mr Gribble if he came out of it, we had no real plans for getting Gran's money back. To track down a thief was one thing, to catch him, another. And we weren't even efficient as spies! We had been turned out of the shrubbery like a lot of silly kids because we hadn't the wit to keep our voices down.

We *were* silly kids. There was nothing we could do!

'I'm off,' I said. I felt, all at once, so angry that I couldn't bear to stay another minute. Angry with Sid, because he was the sort of person who is always full of grand ideas and plans but never does anything when it comes to the point, and angrier still with myself. Since I had known Sid long enough to know he was 'all talk and no do,' as Gran would say, I should have made my own plans for dealing with Mr Gribble, and not relied on him.

I was in such a bad temper and pedalling so hard to work it off, that I must have taken a couple of wrong turnings. I found myself in a short close, lined on both sides and blocked at the end with snug little houses. I turned back into what seemed an unfamiliar road, and cycled slowly along, looking for landmarks. Feeling rather stupid, I remembered that it was Algy who had memorised the directions Sid gave us for finding Lilac Lodge. I had just followed him without noticing where we were going and now, on my own, I was lost in this maze of dark, tree-lined streets, all so much alike that I wondered how the people found their way back to their own homes at night.

There was no one about to ask. Thurston Park was so empty and quiet that it was almost as if the inhabitants were hibernating for the winter. I had decided that I would have to knock at one of the houses, when I turned a corner and saw, at the far end of the next street, a man walking towards me.

I cycled to meet him. He passed under a lamp post and I saw his face. It was Mr Gribble.

CHAPTER EIGHT

BURGLARS AT LILAC LODGE

THIS IS THE point in the story where you usually write, 'I was rooted to the spot with terror.' But you need time to be frightened, and I didn't have time. Nor can you be 'rooted to the spot' when you are riding a bicycle. So I did what in fact turned out to be the sensible thing: I went on riding towards him. It wasn't brave, or stupid: it wasn't anything. I didn't think. I *couldn't* think. It was if my brain had frozen. I just rode on as if I was a clockwork toy that had been wound up and couldn't stop.

And of course he barely glanced at me. Why should he? I was just any boy on a bike. We drew level and then I shot past, pedalling with my head down and a choking tightness in my throat. When I reached the corner of the street, I jammed on my brakes, almost fell off my bike, and looked over my shoulder. He was striding steadily on without looking back, his raincoat flapping, his feet swishing through the crisp fallen leaves.

'You brainless gorm,' a quiet voice said—and my heart bounced like a ball in my chest.

It was Sid. They were all there, lurking in the shadow round the corner.

'Did he recognize you?' Rosie hissed.

I shook my head. I seemed to have no breath to speak.

'He came out of the house just after you went,' Sid said, whispering, though Mr Gribble was well out of earshot now, at the far end of the street. 'He didn't take any notice of us, just walked straight past. We're trailing him . . .'

Mr Gribble had disappeared round the corner.

'Off you go, Algy,' Sid said.

Algy leapt on his bike and tore up the road. Sid put his hand on my handlebars. 'Careful,' he warned. 'We don't want to go after him like a pack of hounds. It'll only scare him. Let Algy tail him, we'll tail *Algy*. Keep well behind, out of sight.

Sid was slow because he had Clio on his crossbar and Rosie because of her ridiculous little bike. I stopped and waited for them at the corner, keeping in the shadow of the hedge. Mr Gribble glanced back once, but all he could have seen in that quiet street was Algy, meandering along and whistling tunelessly, like a boy with plenty of time and nothing on his mind. This street led into the broad, main road: I could see the yellow sodium lights. As soon as Mr Gribble reached it, we jumped on our bikes and raced after him.

The main road was busy. There were plenty of cars and people. A bus roared past us and stopped a little way along, by an arcade of shops. Mr Gribble began to run. He reached the bus just before it moved off, and swung himself on to the platform.

The bus gathered speed, Algy behind it. Head down and pedalling like a madman, he was sucked along in the slipstream.

'That's a terribly dangerous thing to do,' Rosie gasped beside me. Perched on her little bike, her black hair flying, she looked like a witch on a broomstick.

'What *would* his mother say?' I grinned at her and left her behind as I switched into top gear. Though I went as fast as I could, the bus went faster. Algy dwindled to a black speck behind it. By the time I reached the main street of Milton, there was no sign of it and no sign of Mr Gribble either. Only Algy, gesticulating wildly in front of the Odeon cinema.

'He's gone to the pictures!' he panted.

'Probably a blind,' I said. 'Stay here, wait for the others.'

I dropped my bike and raced round the alley at the side of the cinema where there was an exit into the car park. There was no one there. I stationed myself by the door and waited. After a minute or two, Algy joined me. 'Got any money?' he said. 'I'm going inside to see what he's up to. If he's really settled in, watching the film, we've got nearly four hours.'

'What for?'

'Why, to get your Gran's money back, of course.' Algy spoke calmly, as if this was something quite obvious and simple that he had just decided to do. 'The woman in the box office says the cinema's almost empty, so it shouldn't be hard to find him.'

I felt in my pockets. Two safety pins, a sucked piece of chewing gum, a penknife, a couple of shrivelled conkers, a sixpence and a threepenny bit.

'That'll do,' Algy said, snatching the coins. 'Clio's got some.'

And he was gone, leaving me alone in the alley. The exit door swung open and I turned up my jacket collar and stuck my bottom teeth in front of my top ones to bring my jaw forward and make my face look different. But it was only a couple of old women in high-heeled shoes who teetered past me towards the car park, talking in high silly voices about someone called Joan. A little after that, Rosie came running into the alley. 'Algy's gone in, we're waiting round the front. We've got him *trapped*.'

'It's not much use though, is it?' I said sourly. Now the thrill of the actual chase had worn off, all my depression had come back. I felt dull and hopeless. We might have tracked him down, but what could we do now? We couldn't go to the police because Gran didn't want us to, we couldn't force him to hand over the money, we couldn't do anything. '*And* Algy's going to be late home,' I said. 'It's after half-past six. His mother'll make him stay at home for the rest of the year, I should think.'

'What's the matter with you? Got a stomach ache or something?'

I shook my head.

'What is it, then?'

'Oh, I dunno.' I tried to explain. 'Just that we're going on as if it were a sort of game, I suppose. Making plans and trailing him and that. But we're not really going to *do* anything, are we?'

'I think Algy is,' Rosie said. 'He's got that look—you know—the look he gets when he's going to do something.'

At that moment Algy came flying out of the exit and I saw what she meant. His eyes were shining like lamps and he looked ten times more wide awake than he usually did.

'He's sitting in the circle and eating an ice-cream,' he said. 'I should think he's set till the end of the programme. Better hurry, though, in case he only wants to see one film.'

He shot off round the front of the cinema and rushed up to Sid. When Rosie and I came up, Sid was shaking his head.

'No, we can't,' he said flatly. 'I've already explained. It's *stealing.*'

'All right, then.' Algy took off his spectacles, polished them on the edge of his jacket and put them back. 'You're smarter than I am, Sid, so you're probably right. But I don't care. If it's against the law, then I think the law's wrong. So I'm going back to Lilac Lodge and I'm going to break into Mr Gribble's room.'

Sid drew a deep breath. 'Haven't you any sense? Algy—you *pea-brain*. I've explained and explained. Don't you ever *listen?*'

'I listen. But all you ever do is talk.' Algy's mouth had gone stubborn. He looked at us all. 'You needn't come, any of you. I'll go by myself.'

'I want to come,' Clio said. '*I'm* not scared!'

'Neither am I,' I said indignantly. 'And it's *my* Gran, so if anyone's going burgling, it's me!' I looked at Clio. 'And it's all very well to say you're coming, but who do you think's going to lug you back all that way on his bike?'

'You,' Clio said simply. She put her head on one side and smiled. It was the first nice smile she had ever given me. 'You will won't you, Fred?'

Rosie sighed. She looked unhappy—I suppose because she usually sided with Sid. 'I suppose we'd better go now if we're going,' she said.

We all looked at Sid. 'You know what I think,' he said. 'I think it's a daft idea. Plain potty. And I'm not going to have anything to do with it.'

He spoke firmly, but he had gone white. It was a bad moment for him, and we knew it. He had always been the leader in everything we did and now we were turning against him. I think we all felt uncomfortable as we wheeled our bikes down the road—the front of the Odeon cinema being too public to plan a robbery—and left him behind. I glanced back once and he was standing quite still and staring after us. He looked very small and lonely and I felt sad, suddenly. In a funny way, I think it was one of the saddest moments of my life.

At the end of the line of shops there was a patch of waste land, shielded by hoardings. We wheeled our bikes on to it.

'First thing,' Rosie said. 'How's everyone fixed at home? I'm all right, so's Clio. Her Auntie's out and I told my Mum I was staying with her tonight.'

'Mine won't worry,' I said. 'Not till about ten, anyway. I usually go to my Gran, Fridays. But Algy's late home already.'

We looked at him. He was pale. 'I don't care,' he said. 'I just don't *care*.'

'You've got to ring up, though,' I said. 'If you don't, she might get on to the police. That wouldn't be such a bright idea at the moment, would it?'

Algy didn't reply for a moment. Then he said, 'Anyone got a threepenny bit?'

'You cleaned me out, going into the pictures,' Clio said. Rosie and I shook our heads. 'I'll have to reverse the charges, then,' Algy said. He marched off to the telephone box in the main road, head high and shoulders back. He looked like a brave man about to face a firing squad.

We followed him and stood round the telephone box. He

gave us a shaky grin as he spoke to the operator and then turned his back so we couldn't see his face. His hand was holding the receiver so tight that the knuckles stood out in white lumps.

It seemed ages before he put the telephone down. He stood still for a minute, then came slowly out of the box. His forehead was sweaty, but he was smiling.

'What did she say?'

He shrugged his shoulders. 'Nothing that matters. I just told her I was going to the pictures and if she made a fuss about it, I'd leave school the minute I was fifteen and get a job as an errand boy.' His smile grew broader. 'Then I just banged the phone down,' he said.

Clio didn't look heavy, but she was an awful weight on my crossbar. No one spoke as we rode back to Lilac Lodge; we were all thinking too hard. At least, I was. Now we were actually going to do something, I was feeling pretty scared: Sid was almost certainly right about the legal position. And on top of thieving, we were planning to break into someone's house. That was worse than just trespassing, as we did on Death Wall. It was Breaking and Entering.

To stop myself losing my nerve, I made myself think about Gran and how she had been the last time I had seen her—quiet and sad and sort of shut up inside herself. And how the worst thing Mr Gribble had done was not just pinching her money, though that was bad enough, but acting so that Gran had come to like and trust him and then letting her down. Getting the money back wouldn't make Gran feel any happier about that part of it, of course, but it would stop her having to worry about the bills as well: the extra electricity for Mr Gribble's room and the money she owed at the Health Store.

When we stopped outside the gate of Lilac Lodge, I said, 'If anyone's going to break in, it's going to be me.'

Algy started to protest, but Rosie stopped him. 'First thing is, we've got to take a good look at the house and not make any noise. Mr Gribble may be safe at the pictures but there are plenty of other men in the house and we don't want to land up in prison.'

'I don't care,' Algy said.

Rosie looked at him. 'Don't be more of a fool that you can help, Algy Beecham. *You* may not care, but I do, and so do Fred and Clio, I daresay.'

'Kids don't get sent to prison anyway,' I said. 'They go to Reform Schools.'

Algy looked suitably crushed. He said, pleadingly, 'But I don't want to be left out, Fred. You always leave me out when there's anything important to do.'

There was some truth in this. The trouble with Algy is not only that he's clumsy and falls over things, but that he gets carried away. For example, the way he rushed to rescue Aristotle was quite heroic in one sense but in another it was pretty stupid: we managed to escape from old Puffer, but we might not have done. Algy acts first and thinks afterwards which means he's a good person to have around in an emergency—if someone fell into a flooded river, Algy would dive straight in without worrying in case he drowned himself—but if you have to do something which needs thought and planning, give me Sid every time. I know that I wished he was with us at that moment, and not just because he knew Lilac Lodge better than we did. Rosie is sensible enough, but I needed someone to help me hold Algy back and to stop Clio losing her head and giggling.

She started giggling now. 'The Committee ought to have a different name,' she said. 'We ought to call ourselves the Thieves' Committee.' Her cheeks were red with excitement and her eyes were sparkling and her voice rang out hideously clear in the quiet street.

'If you don't shut up we'll be the Prisoners' Committee.' I said. 'We've got to be *quiet*. Clio, you stay here and if anyone comes in the gate, you warn us. Hoot like an owl, or something.'

'I can't hoot,' she said.

'Sing, then. You've got a good, loud voice. Just walk along and sing as if you were going home and singing to keep yourself company. Then it'll look quite natural.'

She didn't look very pleased at being left behind, but she agreed to stay. The rest of us crept up the drive. I went first, then Algy—so close that I could feel his breath on my neck. The house looked big and black against the sky. There were a couple of lights in rooms on the top floor.

The window Sid had pointed out as Mr Gribble's, was to the right of the porch on the first floor. There was enough moonlight to see that it was a sash window and it was open a crack at the bottom. There was a drainpipe running down the side of the porch in just the right place, but when I touched it, it rattled loose: a squirrel might have climbed up it, but not a boy.

The only way up was the porch. It had a sloping glass roof that looked pretty treacherous, but the wood between the panes might be solid enough and, where the roof met the wall above, there was a ledge. If someone stood on the ledge and reached sideways and upwards, he should be able to reach Mr Gribble's window sill and pull himself up on to it.

We measured the distance from the porch with our eyes. 'It'll have to be me,' Algy whispered, in a tone of some satisfaction. 'I'm the only one tall enough.'

Rosie and I exchanged glances. The thought of Algy prancing about on that glass roof was enough to make the blood run cold.

'Let me try first,' I said. 'It's only fair, really. After all, it's *my* Gran. If I can't reach, then you can have a go. Meantime, you wait at the bottom in case I fall and keep an eye on the front door. They'll put a light on in the hall before they come out, probably, so there'll be time to warn me.'

It was easy getting up the porch. There was a sill where the brick ended and the glass began, then a gutter which was firm enough to hold me as I hauled myself up, and the actual roof was quite a lot flatter than it looked from below. But when I reached the ledge, I found Algy was right. I could reach Mr Gribble's sill but I wasn't tall enough to get a proper purchase over the window ledge.

I was stretched out, spread-eagled against the wall, when Clio began to sing. She sang *God Save The Queen*, which was rather a queer choice I thought afterwards—I mean, it's not the sort of song you'd just break into casually as you skipped along the road—but at the time, of course, I didn't think anything. I just froze where I was.

Below me, Algy said, 'Fred, did you hear that?' in much too loud a voice.

'Shut *up*,' I whispered.

'Can you get down, Fred? Someone's coming . . .'

'There's no time. I'm all right. You and Rosie cut along. *Hide*.'

I pressed myself flat against the wall and shut my eyes, hoping that if I stayed absolutely still I would look, in the dark and to a casual glance, like a drainpipe or an overflow or something. It was a pretty feeble hope, but the only possible one in the circumstances. I heard Rosie's gasp as she ran across the lawn to the shrubbery and Algy's feet as he thudded after her—sounding, to my horrified ears, more like an elephant crashing along at full tilt than a running boy.

Then there was silence, and in the silence Clio's voice rose up sweet and clear. 'Frustrate their enemies, confound their *knavish* tricks . . .' And, as her voice died away I heard the creak and whirr of a bicycle coming up the drive. It stopped below me and someone began to cough. It wasn't an ordinary cough, but a long, tormented, wheezing sound that was horrible to listen to and made me hold my breath in sympathy.

When it was over I could hear the harsh note of his breathing, the clatter as he leaned his bike against the wall, and a few seconds later, the juddering slam as he closed the front door.

I stayed still for a minute. I felt stiff as a frozen fish and my fingers were so tangled up in the ivy that grew over the front of the house, that I was sure I would never be able to get them loose. Then Rosie whistled softly below me and I uncurled my fingers very slowly and cautiously and lowered myself onto the roof of the porch. Her face was a pale blur, turned up towards me.

'That was old Puffer,' she whispered. 'He didn't look up. I expect he was coughing too much.'

I crouched on my heels, trying not to put too much weight on the gutter. 'What's he come back for? Why isn't he at the site?'

'Gone sick, I should think. He's got a dreadful cough. It made my stomach hurt to hear him.'

Algy came creeping with elaborate caution across the lawn. 'Light's gone on at the top of the house. That's his room, probably.'

'Maybe he'll go straight to bed,' I said. 'Let's hope so, anyway. But we better be quick before anyone else comes. You'll have to do it, Algy, I can't reach.'

Algy's face lit up and he made a grab at the drainpipe at the side of the porch. It came away with a clang.

'*Careful*,' I said. 'Look—if you're going to do this, you've got to do what I tell you. Put a foot on the ledge at the top of the brick part and a hand on the wall—don't *touch* that drainpipe again, you gormless fool—now heave up and give me the other one.'

A minute later, I had Algy on the roof of the porch. He clutched at me and I almost lost my balance. He was grinning all over his face.

'If we go through this roof, we'll have to pay for it,' I said, which seemed to sober him up more than the thought of getting caught would have done. He went over the roof quite nimbly and we stood on the ledge just below the window. I explained what he had to do, which was to keep his feet on the ledge until he had got his arm through the window up to his armpit. Then—and only then—would it be safe to swing himself away from the ledge and use his other arm to push the lower part of the sash window high enough to let his body through. It was the sort of thing much easier to do than to explain. I would have given a lot at that moment to be tall enough to do it myself: as it was, all I could do was to stand there and watch Algy make a frightful mess of the whole operation.

In fact, I couldn't bear to watch him. I closed my eyes. Rosie told me afterwards that there was one point when his feet slipped off the wall and he just hung, dangling by one arm. He must have made a superhuman effort to recover himself because when I finally made myself open my eyes, he was standing out from the wall in a V like a steeplejack, and pushing the bottom of the window up. It made a creaking sound and something—a bat, I think—flew out from the ivy. Then Algy gave a gasp and hurled himself forward so that his top half was inside and his long legs waving about loose, like a spider's.

They went stiffer and came together as he got his stomach over the window ledge and dived forward. Then he appeared right way up, grinning down at me and holding out his hand. I grabbed it and was through the window in less time than it takes to tell.

The window was in an alcove with curtains across it. They were thick and tightly drawn together which was why we hadn't noticed before that there was a light on. It was a small bedside lamp with a pink shade that had been burned at some time: there was a brown mark on one side of it.

'Wasting electricity,' I said. My Mum carries on like anything if anyone leaves a light burning when they're not in the room.

'I expect he just forgot,' Algy said.

We looked round. It was a medium-sized room and it felt colder than out of doors. The walls were covered with baskets of pink roses except for one corner where the damp had come in and made a brown stain, rough at the edges like a map. There was a wardrobe and a chest of drawers and a wickerwork chair with orange cushions. The bed was high and narrow and looked lumpy.

'Where's he put the money, do you think?' Algy whispered.

'In the drawers—under the mattress . . . We'd better start looking.'

We started on the drawers. They were stuffed full of shirts and underclothes and though we began by being tidy and putting things back when we had looked underneath them, it took too much time and in the end we just took the clothes out, shook them to see if the money was hidden inside, and dropped them on the floor. The funny thing was that I didn't feel in the least scared, and I don't think Algy did either.

There was no money in the drawers. We tipped the mattress off the bed to look underneath it. 'People make slits and put things inside,' Algy said.

It was an old mattress, the ticking was stained and worn in places, but there were no signs of anyone having cut it open recently and stitched it up again. 'You try the bedside table,' I said, and went to open the wardrobe. There were two suits hanging there and a couple of pairs of trousers. I pushed them aside and saw a canvas grip on the floor of the wardrobe. I looked at it. Mr Gribble had a suitcase, a proper, hard-topped suitcase: I remembered it, banging against his legs the day Sid and I had seen him arrive at my Gran's. I thought, *oh well, perhaps he's got rid of it*, and was bending down to get hold of the grip when Algy said, 'Fred, oh Fred . . .'

I straightened up. He was staring at the bedside table.

'What's the matter?' He didn't answer, so I went over to him.

'Look . . .' he said, in a shaking voice.

Beside the pink-shaded lamp there was a glass of water and

in the bottom of the glass there was a set of teeth: white, even teeth with shiny, pale pink gums. They looked as if they were grinning at us, and I snorted with laughter.

Algy turned on me. 'Be *quiet*, this isn't his *room*.' I stared at him and he added frantically, 'He wouldn't have gone to the pictures without his *teeth*.'

'Perhaps he's got two pairs.' I was still, for some curious reason, not frightened at all. 'Weekdays and Sundays,' I said, grinning, but Algy didn't grin back. He wasn't looking at me, but over my shoulder, and his face was a frozen mask of terror.

I turned and saw a man in the doorway. He was wearing a dressing gown and carrying a towel over his arm. The teeth clearly belonged to him because his mouth was all puckered up without them.

CHAPTER NINE

'GRIBBLE, GRIBBLE, WHO'S MR GRIBBLE?'

FOR A MOMENT, I think, he was almost as frightened as we were. Then, realising I suppose that we were too young to be dangerous, his face seemed to tighten up.

'*Got* you,' he said.

Algy gave a little moan. 'Stay where you are,' the man shouted, 'Don't you dare move.' His voice sounded mumbly and blurred. His eyes fixed on Algy. 'Gi' me that.'

Algy looked down at his hands as if surprised to find they belonged to him. He was holding a red leather wallet: he must have been going through the drawers in the bedside table when he caught sight of the teeth. He gave another moan and tossed the wallet in the man's direction. He caught it, glanced at the contents quickly and stuffed it in his pocket. He said, 'Stan' over there. Quick sharp now.'

He gestured and we stood together in the corner. The man advanced on us. I put up my arm to shield my face but he wasn't intending to hit us, not at the moment, anyway. He took the teeth out of the glass, popped them in his mouth and champed them into place. He took glasses out of his dressing gown pocket and put them on. I recognised him now. He was the man who had turned us out of the garden.

His eyes roamed the room and my heart sank. It looked a terrible mess, clothes all over the floor, the mattress half off the bed. Then he looked at us. 'Caught in the act,' he said, speaking more clearly now he had his teeth in. 'Weren't satisfied last time, I suppose.'

What last time? I hadn't the courage to ask.

'The cheek of it!' His face seemed to be swelling up; blobs of scarlet appeared on his cheekbones. 'The cheek of it!' he repeated, the words bubbling out of his mouth as if something were boiling over inside him. 'Coming back bold as brass!'

There were footsteps outside the room and he went to the door and shouted, 'Jelly—that you? Come here a minute.'

Jelly was short and fat and he wore a striped shirt without a collar. His braces dangled loose and his stomach hung over his trousers, wobbling as he came in. *Wibble, wobble, wibble, wobble, jelly on a plate.* That was what we used to sing after fat people when I was smaller: in any other circumstances, the coincidence would have made me laugh.

Mr Jelly looked round the room. 'Quite a party! What's the trouble, Mr Stanley?'

Mr Stanley said, 'You know I lost that ten quid this morning? Well, I've caught them this time. Red-handed. Couple of young thugs.'

'Goodness me,' Mr Jelly said. 'Oh, my goodness!' His mouth was a rosy, round O of surprise.

'Sir' Algy stammered. 'S-sir—we've not been here before. *Honestly.*'

'Tell that to your grandmother! Jelly, do me a favour, will you, and ring the police?' He seemed less angry now, almost cheerful, as if he were enjoying himself. I wondered if we could rush at them and get through the door. Mr Stanley was tall but he didn't look particularly strong, and Mr Jelly was much too fat to chase after us. If we took them by surprise . . .

Then I saw it was no good. I had often planned what we could do if we were trapped by desperate criminals, how we could outwit them and escape by cunning, but this situation was one I had never thought of. *We* were the criminals, caught red-handed as Mr Stanley had said. Even if we told the truth, which we couldn't do because of Gran, they would never believe us. I thought, *this isn't happening, it isn't true.* I knew that Algy was feeling much the same: his mouth hung open and he was blinking his eyes rapidly as if he were in the middle of a bad dream and trying to wake up.

'Better get hold of someone else, hadn't I?' Mr Jelly said.

'Don't fancy leaving you alone with them. Might turn nasty—they *look* pretty nasty to me. Probably got razors or something.'

'FitzWilliam's in,' Mr Stanley said. 'I heard him coughing while I was having my bath.'

'I'll fetch him.' Mr Jelly backed away, keeping his eyes on us as if we were dangerous animals. 'Leave the door open, Stanley, then I'll hear if you call.'

We heard the flip-flop of his slippers as he climbed the stairs and the thud of his knuckles on a door and then the rumble of voices talking. Flip-flop down the stairs again. Then his round, grinning face in the doorway. 'He'll be down soon as he's dressed. I'll 'phone the police now.'

He went on, down the stairs to the hall. We heard the *ting* as he picked up the telephone.

Algy said, 'Sir—Mr Stanley—*please*, Sir, it's true what I said. We've not been here before, not in your room. Only in the . . .'

'*Algy*,' I said, but I was too late.

' . . . only in the garden,' Algy finished and then, immediately, realised what he had done. His eyes widened with horror.

There was a short silence. We could hear Mr Jelly talking in the hall, though not what he said. And then another *ping* as he put the receiver down. Mr Stanley looked at us. His face was puzzled for a minute and then he said, 'I thought I'd seen you before. You're the kids who were snooping round earlier on. Where are the others?'

'At home,' I said quickly. 'We're on our own, honest we are.'

'Are you now? We'll see about that.' He strode to the door and called softly, 'Jelly, you there? Take a look in the grounds, will you?'

Algy gasped and made for the window. But before he could reach it and cry out a warning, Mr Stanley caught his arm and hit him across the face. Algy's eyes filled with tears. He put the back of his hand to his lips. It came away flecked with blood.

'You'll get worse than that if you make any noise,' Mr Stanley said. 'Now.' He looked at us steadily. 'You might as well tell me. What did you do with my ten quid?'

Algy said frantically, 'Mr Gribble took it, sir!' He clutched at me. 'Fred, don't you see?' I gaped at him, only half aware of what he was saying because I was listening for sounds from outside. If Clio did what she'd been told, and waited by the gate, she'd be safe enough. But would she have waited? I heard the front door slam and strained my ears. 'Don't you remember?' Algy went on, almost crying now. 'Sid saw him in this room, that's why we thought it was Mr Gribble's, and when he saw Sid, he dodged back. Sid said it was a guilty conscience, he *meant* about your Gran, but it was really because he was stealing . . .'

'Gribble, Gribble, who's Mr Gribble?' Mr Stanley looked bewildered and angry. 'I've had enough,' he said impatiently. 'You can spin your yarns to the police, I don't want to hear them.'

'But Mr Stanley . . .'

'Do you want me to clout you again?'

Algy shivered and pressed close to me. His mouth was still bleeding. For a while—it couldn't have been long, really, but it seemed like hours—we stood in silence, Mr Stanley watched us, a cold gleam in his eye.

Then, suddenly, we heard a scream, and Clio's voice. 'Let me go, *lemme go* . . .' She didn't sound frightened, just furious. 'Lemme go you beast, you fat, horrible, smelly beast . . .'

We stood, petrified. Her cries came nearer, up the stairs, along the passage. Then she appeared. Mr Jelly was holding her by the back of her jersey; his other hand clutched Rosie's wrist. Clio was wriggling and shouting and, as he dragged her into the room, she twisted her head round and sunk her teeth into his forearm. He squawked and let go. 'Little hell cat,' he said. He rubbed at his arm and his fat face was scarlet. 'Tell you what, Stanley, we ought to give these kids a real good hiding before the police come. That's what they need, a good, sharp lesson they won't forget!'

Clio bolted to our corner and stood beside me. 'If you touch me I'll scream,' she said. Her face was as red as Mr Jelly's. 'I'll scream and scream and *scream*.'

'I'll give you something to scream for, then,' Mr Jelly said, and suddenly began to grin in the most horrible way.

'Oh, give over, Jelly,' Mr Stanley said. 'They're only kids.' He sounded a little uncomfortable and it seemed to give Rosie courage. She hadn't made a sound since Jelly had hauled her in. She looked pale and much more scared than Clio, probably because she had enough sense to realise that there was no point in yelling and being indignant because, on the face of it, anyway, we were terribly in the wrong.

She looked up at Mr Stanley. 'We're not thieves, really we're not. I know it looks like that, but it's not true. We were just trying to get something back. Something Mr Gribble stole from someone we knew.'

'It's no good, Rosie,' I said despairingly. 'You see, this isn't Mr Gribble's room, so they won't believe us.'

'But it must be. Sid said it was!' She sounded astonished, as if it was a law of nature that Sid should always be right about everything. It made me so angry that I forgot everything else for the moment.

'Well, Sid was wrong for once, wasn't he?' I said heatedly. 'He just said he saw Mr Gribble at the window. It was just a *guess*.'

Rosie turned on me, white-faced. 'That's what you say now, Clever Dick, you didn't think of it before, did you?'

'Algy did. Only Sid slapped him down the way he always does. You know what he's like. Algy said . . . '

'WHO IS MR GRIBBLE?' Mr Stanley roared. 'For Pete's sake—what d'you think this is? A school debating society? This is my room, it was my ten quid, what's Mr Gribble got to do with it?'

'He lives here,' I said. 'He used to live with my—with this person he stole from. But he lives here now.'

Mr Stanley looked at Mr Jelly. 'Make sense to you?'

'No one by that name here. Never has been, far as I know.'

'But there *must* be,' I cried. 'You must believe us, really. He stole from this—this friend of our's and then he ran away and we tracked him here. And this other friend of our's saw him at your window this morning, that's why we thought it was his room, but he must have just crept in here, stealing your money . . .'

Mr Stanley took off his glasses, wiped them on his dressing gown and put them back. His face was wary but I had the feeling that he almost believed me. And I think he might have believed me altogether, in the end, if old Puffer hadn't come snorting and snuffling along the corridor and entered the room.

Old Puffer, of course, was Mr FitzWilliam. He looked ill and smelt of camphorated oil. He said, between coughs, that he was sorry he'd been so long, but he'd been in bed and it had taken him a while to get up again. He looked at us while Mr Stanley and Mr Jelly told him what we had done. Or what they believed we had done.

'I'm not surprised,' Puffer wheezed, holding his side as if it hurt him to talk. 'They're a bad lot, I know 'em. Running wild, trespassing on the factory grounds—no decent homes to go to, I suppose. And this isn't the first time they've been up to something. They've got a whole pile of loot tucked away in an old car down on the site. Not that I thought they'd stolen it when I first saw it, mind, it looked more like some kind of kid's game to me . . .'

He looked so dreadful, his poor old face so yellow and hollowed-out with coughing, that I couldn't help remembering how we had teased him with Aristotle and shouted after him and made him run. I felt too sorry and ashamed to explain about the jumble in the car, and I could see by their faces that the others did too. Even Clio looked red and miserable—so miserable that I forgot how awful she was. I took her hand and squeezed it to comfort her, but it didn't seem to: instead tears welled up in her eyes and spilled slowly down her cheeks. Algy gave her his handkerchief.

'Kid's game?' Mr Jelly snapped. 'Stuff and nonsense, Fitz. Never seen a guiltier looking lot in my life! Bunch of thieving brats, that's what they are . . .'

I don't remember much after that, until the policeman came. We just stood there, huddled close, and Clio went on crying.

Jinny says I should describe what happened next, but I can't. The truth is, I only remember bits here and there, like snapshots. I don't even know what the policeman looked like; all I remember is staring at the middle of his blue uniform jacket as he asked my name and then the feel of his hand on my shoulders as we all went down the stairs. Then the crunch of our feet on the gravel and the look of the lamplight shining on the brown leaves on the pavement and the cold feel of the car seat behind my knees as we drove to the station. I wondered what would happen to our bikes, but I didn't dare say anything.

At the station there was a bright light over the desk and the policeman behind it had a grey and ginger moustache and enormous lumpy ears with hairs growing out of them. I remember looking at his ears as he asked us our names and I remember Algy's face as he gave his. It was sick and shocked and his nose was running. Quite a kind voice said, 'Got a hanky, son?' and he put his hand in his pocket in a slow, dazed way and then shook his head.

Someone said, 'You've got to wait in here. The Inspector'll want a word with you later.'

'Here' was a room with chairs and a table and posters on the walls. There was one of Ramsgate with a ram jumping over a gate and yellow sands and blue sky behind. I wondered if they always hung advertisements for seaside places on the walls of police stations and prisons, to remind people of what they had left behind outside.

The policeman who had shown us into the room said, 'Cheer up, they've abolished capital punishment in this country,' and closed the door.

We sat down on the chairs, in a straight line against the wall. We sat still, our hands dangling. Then, very slowly, we looked at each other.

Algy said, 'I wish I were dead. I'd rather be dead than this.'

It sounded awful. Clio began to cry again and Rosie put an arm round her and said, 'You'll have to tell about your Gran, Fred.'

'It won't make any difference. They'll never believe us. You heard what Mr Jelly said? Mr Gribble doesn't live there.'

'They'll send for our parents,' Rosie said. 'My Mum'll tell them a thing or two.'

This wasn't, for the rest of us, much comfort. Clio had no parents to send for, mine wouldn't exactly dance with joy at the news that their only son was a criminal, caught in the act, and as for Algy—well, perhaps he was right: he would be better dead.

'I'll kill myself,' Algy said. 'I'll cut my veins.'

'Oh, don't be such a fabulous nit,' Rosie said, but without much conviction.

I said, 'I don't suppose they make you do homework in prison.' It was the only thing I could think of to cheer him up, and it did, but only for a minute.

He smiled and then the smile vanished from his face as if it had been wiped off. 'I've got to face *them* first, haven't I?' He relapsed into gloom and stared at his wrists.

Rosie said, 'I don't understand why they said Mr Gribble doesn't live there. We saw him come out.'

I had forgotten that. 'Are you sure?' I tried to think back. 'I mean, we'd all walked down the road a bit, to collect our bikes, hadn't we?'

'Then you lost your temper and rode off . . .' I didn't like this description of my behaviour, but as Rosie hadn't said it to be nasty, only to try and remember what had actually happened, I let it pass.

'Did you go back to Lilac Lodge after that? If you didn't, I can't see how you can be certain he came out of that gate, and not another one.'

Rosie looked harassed. 'No—we didn't go back. I can't really remember, it all happened so quickly. I think we just turned and saw him. And Sid said . . .'

'Oh, Sid's always right, isn't he?' I said sarcastically.

'I hate Sid,' Clio said, through her tears. 'I just hate and despise him. He's a horrible, mean *traitor.*'

'He was right, though,' Rosie said miserably. 'I mean he told us not to do it.'

Algy lifted his head and said slowly, 'Sid was right about Mr Gribble, too. I think you're being too clever, Fred. Of course he lives in Lilac Lodge and of course he pinched Mr Stanley's money. After all, Sid saw him at Mr Stanley's window and then he was sure he saw him come out of the house. He might have made a mistake once, but he couldn't have made a mistake *twice.* It would be too much of a coincidence.' He paused for a minute. 'I expect Mr Gribble's just changed his name,' he said.

We looked at him almost with awe. For a minute, it seemed so simple, so obvious. We were filled with relief and excitement. Clio dried her eyes and Rosie was smiling. 'Good old Algy,' I said, and he looked modestly pleased, pushing his glasses up on his nose and grinning quietly.

Then, suddenly, my heart sank. This was something I had read about in books but I had never really felt it happen to me before. It was just as if my heart had turned into a solid lump and dropped down to my stomach, leaving a hollow, aching space behind.

'It's no good,' I said. 'Since we don't know what he's changed it *to*. No one'll listen to us. Why should they? We haven't any *evidence*. We may know Mr Gribble's a thief, but all they know is that *we* are. We're burglars—criminals, caught in the act!'

Clio began to cry again, softly and despairingly. None of us tried to comfort her. There wasn't any comfort we could think of.

I don't know how long we waited there. I sat and stared at the poster of sunny Ramsgate. My head was aching and after a little while, it seemed to me as if the room was actually growing smaller. As if the prison walls were closing in upon us all.

CHAPTER TEN

A VISIT TO THE CINEMA

THE DOOR OPENED and a policeman said, 'Come along now.'
We got up slowly and followed him. There was the entrance
hall and the desk and the policeman with the moustache and the
ears. As we passed, he grinned at us, which surprised me. On
the other side of the vestibule there was a door standing open
and we could see a desk with a man in an ordinary suit sitting
behind it.

'Bring in the desperadoes, Sergeant Andrews,' he said. Clio
gasped beside me and clutched my hand.

We went in. There were other people in the room but I was
so scared I daren't look at them: I only saw them out of the
corner of my eye, like shadows. We stood in a line in front of
the Inspector's desk and he looked at us each in turn. He had
blue eyes with brown flecks in them, and bristly eyebrows like
old, splayed-out toothbrushes.

'Well,' he said. 'You've got a lot of explaining to do,
haven't you?'

Someone made a sound and I looked and saw my Gran. She
was sitting in a chair at the side of the room and Sid was
standing beside her and beside Sid was his Uncle William,
looking enormous in a large, hairy overcoat.

'Gran!' I said. She smiled at me but shook her head at the
same time in a warning way, and looked at the Inspector.

He cleared his throat. 'Now. You four. I've heard a very
unfortunate story about your behaviour tonight. The fact that
your friends here have come to speak on your behalf, doesn't
altogether explain it. You broke into a house and were caught
stealing a wallet from Mr Stanley's room . . .'

'We thought it was Mr Gribble's,' Algy burst out.

The Inspector frowned. 'So I understand. But what has that

got to do with it? As far as the police are concerned, you made an illegal entry into a private house with the intention of stealing. To say you were taking the law into your own hands, is no excuse at all.'

'It was my fault,' Gran said. Her eyes were very bright. She was wearing her old seal-skin cape which Mum was always trying to make her throw away because it was bald in places, and her best hat, a black hat with shiny, purple feathers. She must have put it on in a hurry because it had slipped crooked and her hair showed in cottony wisps beneath it. Gran tried to push her hat straight and her fingers were trembly. 'I didn't want anyone to know what an old fool I'd been, I made them promise. I should never have done that!'

'You mustn't blame yourself, Mrs Blackadder. While it might have been more sensible to come straight to us, you couldn't have guessed they would do what they did. And it is *what* they did that concerns the police! I don't say the Superintendent won't take what you've told us into consideration when he decides whether or not to proceed with a prosecution. But it may be difficult for him to do so. Innocent people have been concerned, after all. Mr Stanley has not only been put to great inconvenience, but he has lost ten pounds, and we have no real evidence that these young people are not guilty.' He paused. 'If we had—if we could put our hands on the real culprit, now, it might—only *might*, mind you, be a different matter!'

'My Fred wouldn't steal,' Gran burst out.

'I'm afraid that's just what he *was* going to do, Mrs Blackadder,' the Inspector said, very gently.

Algy said, 'Sir . . .'

The Inspector raised one bristly eyebrow.

'Could you ask—I mean, could we find out who the other people in the house are?'

'No one by the name of Gribble, we know *that*. Sergeant Andrews will know of course, he's taking a statement from Mr Stanley now, but I can't see it will help, even if I tell you.'

'P-please Sir,' Algy stammered. 'If he's changed his name we might—well—I mean there might be a *clue*.'

Sid's Uncle William spoke for the first time. 'Last request of the condemned man,' he said. He looked at me and winked as if to say, *cheer up, things aren't as bad as they seem*.

'I suppose there might,' the Inspector said slowly. He looked at Uncle William. 'Keep an eye on them for a minute, then. I don't want to come back and find they've swiped my fountain pen.'

Uncle William laughed uproariously, though it didn't seem to me that the Inspector had said anything particularly funny.

As soon as he had gone, Sid rushed over to us. 'You clots, you absolute ghastly *mental cases* . . .'

'Oh, give over, Sid,' I said. 'How'd you *get* here, that's what we want to know.'

Sid's eyes were shining. 'Well—after you'd gone, I thought, those half-wits are going to get into trouble. Dead trouble. I couldn't think what to do, then I thought—*well*, if they do get caught, someone'll fetch the police and they'll be hauled down to the station. So I went to see Uncle William and he got out his van and we came along and parked outside the station and waited. And then, when you criminal types came along in custody, we followed you in and Uncle William told his chum, Sergeant Andrews—he's the one at the desk with the big ears—what I'd told *him*. And Sergeant Andrews said it would be better if your Gran was here, for evidence about old Gribble, so Uncle William went and fetched her . . .'

'Didn't give me time to put my hat on properly, I must look a fine old sight,' Gran said. She was smiling but it was rather a wavery smile and in spite of everyone watching, I went over and hugged and kissed her.

'I'm sorry, Gran,' I said. 'You must have been awfully upset.'

'Don't worry about me, Fred. I don't often get a bit of excitement like this.' She squeezed me tight and then smiled at me again as she let me go, but there were tears in her eyes.

'And *then*,' Sid said impatiently—he hates being inter-rupted—'then we saw the Inspector and Mr Stanley and old Puffer. And Mr Stanley was quite nice, really, when he heard all about it and old Puffer said he hadn't really thought we were bad kids . . .'

'Poor Mr FitzWilliam,' Gran said. 'I used to know him years ago—he used to give Albert a hand with the picture-framing one time—and I'd no idea he was still alive. I'm surprised he *is* with that chest he's got and living in a damp room doesn't help it, he says . . .'

Algy said abruptly, 'Have they told our parents yet?'

We looked at him. We were all quiet, suddenly, even Sid. We knew—that is, Sid, Rosie and I knew—what this meant to Algy. And Gran and Uncle William must have guessed from the looks on our faces, because Gran said, 'Come on, boy, they can't kill you,' and Uncle William added, uncomfortably, 'I'm afraid they will have to tell them, old chap. No way round it.'

Algy looked despairing and stared at the ground. There was nothing we could say to comfort him, so we just stood round in mournful silence and, when the Inspector came in, he looked at us and said in a kindlier tone than he had used up to now, 'Cheer up now! Sergeant Andrews is going to fetch your parents shortly, you'll soon be tucked up in bed!'

In the circumstances, this was not the jolliest thing to hear. I thought Algy was going to faint, he went so white. I was wondering whether there was any way to explain to the Inspector exactly how awful Algy's parents were, and how telling them what he'd done would be a much worse punish-ment than sending him to prison for ten years would be, when the Inspector began reading a list of names from a paper in his hand. He read rather quickly, as if he didn't believe there was much point in the exercise. 'Mr Amos Thistle, Mr Marcus Jones, Mr Tim Smith, Mr Jelly, Mr Stanley, Mr FitzWilliam. You've met the last three and the others have lived in Lilac

Lodge for years. The only recent arrivals—all within the last fortnight—are Mr Blackstock, Mr Collier'—he was speaking more slowly now—'Mr Hubbel, Mr Ahmed . . .'

'HUBBEL,' I shrieked. The Inspector lowered his list and stared at me. Everyone else was staring too, as if I had suddenly gone raving mad. I could feel my face going hot as fire. 'Gran,' I said. '*Hubbel's Fluid!* That muck he drinks!'

To give credit where it's due, the Inspector was no fool. He didn't waste time asking me to explain but strode to the door and called out to Sergeant Andrews that he wanted to see Mr Stanley and Mr FitzWilliam. When they came in, he almost snapped at them. 'This man Hubbel. What d'you know about him?'

'Arrived just under a week ago,' Mr Stanley said. 'Gloomy fellow.'

'Voice like a foghorn,' old Puffer wheezed.

I jumped up and down. 'Is he a vegetarian?'

Mr Stanley looked at me, and, quite unexpectedly, smiled. 'Can't say, I'm sure.'

Algy said, 'There's one way of finding out if he *is* Mr Gribble.'

'What's that?' The Inspector turned to him so sharply that Algy began to blink with nervousness, but he answered stoutly enough.

'Well, we could look and see. Someone who knows Mr Gribble and someone who knows Mr Hubbel, and if they both recognise him, he's the same man.'

'Ha, ha! Funny fellow,' the Inspector said.

'Algy's not joking,' I cried. '*Our* Mr Gribble's at the pictures. In the Odeon. What's the time?'

The Inspector glanced at his watch. 'A quarter past ten.'

'Then we'd better hurry,' I said, 'he should be coming out any minute now.'

After that, things began to happen very fast. The Inspector

flicked the intercom on his desk and said he wanted a police car brought round straight away. He asked Mr Stanley if he would mind going with him. 'Mr FitzWilliam had better stay in the warm, and Mrs Blackadder, but Fred can come.' He looked at me thoughtfully. 'You'll recognise your grandma's lodger, won't you?'

As you might expect, there was a chorus of objections from the others. 'It's not fair,' 'Why not *me*,' and 'Please, sir, I know what he looks like too!' but the Inspector silenced them. 'What d'you think this is? A school outing?' he said.

Sid whispered something to his Uncle William, who shook his head. But the Inspector must have heard—or guessed—what Sid said because he grinned suddenly. 'Why not?' he said to Uncle William. 'They've earned a bit of excitement. As long as you keep an eye on them, and don't let them get in my way.'

I got in the back of the police car with Mr Stanley. Through the back windows I could see the others, piling into Uncle William's Safe Transit van. Sid waved at me and gave a thumbs-up sign.

I said to Mr Stanley, because it was impossible *not* to say something when we were sitting next to each other, 'I'm sorry we made such an awful muck up in your room.'

He smiled at me. I was reminded of the way his teeth had sat grinning away at us in the glass, and had a terrible struggle not to laugh!

He said, 'I'm sorry, too. It seems I mistook your intentions.' He gave a little cough, as if something was tickling in his throat.

The police car moved off. The police station was about half-a-mile from the Odeon, and we got there just as the last house was beginning to trickle out. We stopped on the opposite side of the road and Uncle William's van stopped a little way behind us. As we got out, I could see the others staring pop-eyed through the windscreen.

The Inspector, Mr Stanley and I, crossed the road.

'Why don't you park outside the cinema?' I asked.

'Because parking isn't allowed that side, and *no one*, neither police, nor boys who fancy themselves as policemen, are allowed to break the law,' the Inspector said. Like some of our masters at school, he was a man for hammering a point home. I sighed heavily and he glanced down at me, it seemed with amusement. 'Besides, we don't want to frighten him off, do we? If you take someone by surprise, he's more likely to come along quietly.'

We stood outside the cinema, next to the sweet machine. For the first time that evening, I realised I hadn't had any tea, and was horribly hungry. My stomach was a great, yawning hole; the water came into my mouth as I looked at the chocolate bars behind the grill.

People were coming out faster now and my hunger vanished. I began to feel sick instead. Suppose he wasn't there after all, suppose he had sneaked out in the middle of the programme and taken a train somewhere—Birmingham, say, or Scotland? There was no reason why he should have done this, since he didn't know we were after him, but when you are in the middle of something exciting, it is not always easy to be reasonable. I had begun to be sure he must have escaped and that we would never find him again, when I saw him.

He was coming down the stairs from the Circle. His raincoat was undone, flapping round him like a cloak, and his long face was pushed forward like a sad dog's. I clutched the Inspector's arm. 'That's him . . .' He was walking across the foyer. The Inspector glanced at Mr Stanley, who nodded.

'Wait here.' The Inspector strolled forward. Mr Gribble was coming down the steps. 'Excuse me, Sir,' the Inspector said. 'I'd like a word with you, if you don't mind.'

He sounded much too casual, much too polite. Suddenly, I had the terrible feeling that he had only half-believed us, that he wasn't, really, taking this very seriously, and that Mr Gribble had only to give another false name—Mr Smith, say—and the Inspector would let him go. It was stupid to think like that, of course, and what I did then was just about the most stupid thing I had ever done in my life, but I couldn't help it. I couldn't bear the thought that he might get away. I rushed forward and shouted, 'It's him, it's *really* him, he stole my Gran's money . . .'

Mr Gribble took one look at me and bolted back into the cinema. The Inspector's face was stoney with anger. 'You fool,' he muttered, and ran after him. Mr Stanley followed. I stood, stunned, and watched them pushing their way up the Circle stairs through the people who were still coming down. I thought—*the exit*—and tore round the side of the Odeon. A queue of cars, edging their way out into the main road, blinded me with their headlights. I stumbled past them and through the door of the exit. For a minute, the stone stairs were empty; then, suddenly, there was the thud of feet and Mr Gribble came flying down, his raincoat spread behind him like a sail. I rushed to stop him but he brushed me aside and I fell heavily on my elbow, jarring the funny bone. At once, the pain was so awful, that it seemed to fill the world. I lay, doubled up on the ground and I could hear myself moaning, but as if it was someone else, a long way off. And then, as the pain began to wear off—which happens quite quickly with banged funny bones—I heard the Inspector's voice. 'Fred—*Fred*, you all right, boy?' I rolled over and saw his grey eyebrows just above me. He said, 'Look after him, Stanley,'—and was gone.

Mr Stanley put his hands under my armpits and helped me up. 'Only my elbow,' I managed to say, 'it's going off now.' I hung on to him and we staggered out of the door and up the alley.

The police car, siren going, had veered across the traffic to our side of the road and the Inspector was running beside it as it slowed to a stop. People were standing and staring. A woman near me, said, 'Oh, I expect it's just something for television, Arthur.' Mr Gribble was nowhere to be seen.

The pain in my arm was much better now and I felt horribly ashamed. If the Inspector hadn't stopped to see if I was all right, he might not have lost Mr Gribble. I saw Mr Stanley looking at me anxiously, and I rubbed my elbow and bit my lip, hoping that he would realise how bad it had been, and not blame me.

A little knot of men had collected round the police car. One of them spoke to the Inspector and pointed up the street. 'That's right,' another said. 'Chap in a great, long raincoat, running as if the devil was after him. Turned into Belmont Road.'

The Inspector turned to us. 'Get in, Stanley. Fred, go to your friends in the van. Tell them to go back to the station.'

'Oh, *Sir* . . .' I began, but his expression stopped me.

'DO AS YOU'RE TOLD,' he bellowed, and got into the car. Mr Stanley got in beside him and the car revved up and shot off like a bullet, screaming up on the wrong side of the road and into the next street on the right.

On the corner of this street was the telephone box from which, earlier on, Algy had telephoned his mother. There was a man in it now: a tall, thin man wearing a dark suit. Almost as soon as the police car had vanished, this man stepped out of the box, looked right, looked left, and crossed the main street, stepping fairly briskly but no more briskly than any other man in a hurry.

It was Mr Gribble. He was carrying his raincoat, neatly folded over one arm. He stood by the bus stop. A bus came down the road and he lifted his hand to stop it.

CHAPTER ELEVEN

'STOP THIEF!'

FOR A SECOND, I couldn't believe it. Then I saw what had happened. He had run into Belmont Road, his raincoat billowing—so much too big for him that it was the one thing about him everyone would notice—then he had simply taken it off and walked back to the telephone box, looking without it and to a casual eye, like a completely different man . . .

I looked frantically round me. The little group of people who had been watching the police car had melted away. Only Sid and Uncle William were watching from the opposite pavement. I stumbled across the road. They ran to meet me and Uncle William caught hold of my arm. I struggled. shouting, 'Let me go, we got to stop him,' though there was really, no chance of that: the bus stop was too far down the road.

'Job for the police,' Uncle William said calmly, relaxing his hold as the bus moved off. 'He's a smart chap, your Mr Gribble. That's the oldest trick in the world, doubling back on your tracks when no one expects you to, but it takes a cool head to do it.'

'It's not *just* a job for the police,' Sid said indignantly. 'It's for everyone to stop a thief. It's your duty as a citizen. Your *legal* duty.'

'Not for minors,' Uncle William said. 'Figure out for yourself what a state of affairs there'd be if every youngster in the country behaved like an amateur detective!' He spoke in a mild, thoughtful way, as if he were sitting by his own fireside enjoying a good discussion and it suddenly struck me that it must be from his uncle's side of the family that Sid got his infuriating habit of arguing about a thing instead of doing it.

About half-a-mile down the road, the traffic lights turned red and the bus slowed down. I shouted, 'We've got to follow him, the Inspector said so,' and ran for the van, hoping that in the heat of the moment it wouldn't occur to Uncle William that the Inspector believed he was following old Gribble himself.

'Come on Uncle Will, you heard what Fred said,' Sid yelled behind me.

We piled into the van. Algy and the girls were in the back with Jake, who growled as I tumbled among them. 'It's all right Fred,' Clio said, 'he won't hurt you.'

'Just keep him in sight,' Sid begged, getting into the front. His uncle, heaving his huge bulk behind the steering wheel, groaned aloud, but he started up the van.

'*Hurry*,' I cried. Ahead, the traffic lights turned green. 'We can catch up if we hurry, there's a bus stop just beyond.'

The van roared along. Lamp posts streaked by in a blur of light. 'If we don't catch him he'll just disappear,' I said. 'Now he knows we've rooted him out . . .'

' Want me to break the speed limit?' Uncle William grumbled, but all the same, peering over his shoulder, I saw the speedometer flicker up to sixty.

We went through the lights as they turned red again. A car, coming out of the side street, hooted angrily. The bus was just moving off from the next stop.

'He didn't get off, just a woman with a suitcase.' Sid was bouncing in his seat with excitement.

'Next stop's the station,' Rosie said. 'The last stop, too. They turn the passengers off and go back to the garage.'

The streets were almost empty now and the bus fairly streaked along, swaying slightly and looking like a lighted ship. It reached the level crossing and bumped as it crossed the sleepers. Then the crossing gates began to close and Uncle William swore under his breath and braked hard, throwing us forward. I bumped my nose on the back of the seat and Jake's paws slithered on the floor of the van.

'It's the Portsmouth Trident' Algy said—he used to go in for train-spotting. 'It stops here and then it goes straight through to Portsmouth.'

We could hear the train now: a distant hum, a wild, sad hoot as it went through the cutting, and then a gathering roar.

'Come on,' Algy gasped and flung open the doors at the back of the van.

'Stay where you are,' Uncle William shouted. 'D'you hear me? If he catches the train, the police'll get him at Portsmouth.'

He grabbed Sid, but he was the only one he could reach. The rest of us jumped out of the back of the van, slammed the doors shut, and with Algy in the lead, pounded up the steps and over the footbridge across the railway line. We rushed down the other side and along the empty platform to the booking hall. Mr Gribble was standing by the ticket office, the light falling full on his face.

We saw him, and, in that same split second, realised there was a barrier between us. A trolley, loaded with mailbags, stood square across the exit from the platform, the tall Jamaican porter behind it. With a roar, the Portsmouth Trident drew into the station. Mr Gribble looked up and his sad eyes met mine. Then he turned and ran, out into the station yard.

'Stop thief,' Algy shouted and began to wriggle past the end of the trolley. A mail bag fell off with a thump. 'Careful now, what's your hurry, boy?' the Jamaican said. 'Train's not due out for another ten minutes.' Algy gave an expiring moan, rather like a balloon when the air is pressed out of it, and squeezed his stomach through the narrow gap. He pushed past the porter and ran on. The Jamaican saw me behind him and a broad grin spread over his face. 'Why, if it isn't the Secret Service! After another spy, are you?' Chuckling, he bent to pick up the mail bag.

I am not fat, but I'm fatter than Algy. I couldn't get past

the trolley. I gasped and flew for the middle of it, trying to leap it like a vaulting horse, but it was too wide. I landed on top of the load, which collapsed beneath me. The nice Jamaican stopped laughing and stood up. 'Watch it,' he shouted and then, in tones of pure disbelief, 'what d'you think you're doing?' as the girls hurled themselves at the mail bags too. For a minute or so, it was utter chaos. One mail bag burst open, letting out a shower of letters and Clio skidded in them, scattering them in all directions; Rosie tripped over another and fell on top of me with a shriek of mixed fear and laughter. We were too tangled up to move. The Jamaican heaved us both to our feet, looking as angry as his cheerful face would allow but he was too startled—and perhaps too gentle—to hold us. We twisted out of his grasp and raced through the booking office and into the station yard.

We were too late. There was no sign of Algy or Mr Gribble. The bus stood there, lighted and empty, but the driver had gone. 'To get a cup of tea, I expect,' Rosie said. 'What shall we do?' Clio asked, a little fearfully.

I looked right, to the brightly lit main road, and left, to the dark railway sidings. 'I don't know . . .' I began, and stopped as a high, thin cry rose up, somewhere on our left, at the far end of the station yard. '*Algy* . . .' I shouted, but even if he had answered we couldn't have heard him because at that moment Uncle William's van swept into the station. It stopped with a squeal of brakes. Uncle William and Sid jumped out, Jake behind them. 'Get back in the van at once,' Uncle William thundered, such a commanding note in his voice and such a purposeful look on his face as he strode towards us, that I was almost hypnotised into obeying him. It was Rosie who said, 'But we can't—Mr Gribble's got Algy.' She tugged at my arm and said in a suddenly shocked way, as if the meaning of that scream had only just got through to her, 'Fred, he might *kill* him . . .'

'What's that . . . ?' Uncle William said sharply, but we had already begun to run. We heard him shouting after us, though not what he said, because the Jamaican porter came out of the station and began yelling at us too!

'What's he saying about mail bags?' Sid panted beside me, but there was no time to explain. We reached the sidings, dodged between the stationary trucks, stumbled over the lines. At the bottom of the yard the brick side of the cutting rose up; above it was the cinder path that led down to the river and Death Wall. There was an iron ladder let into the side of the cutting and, lying beside it, a Milton High School blazer, folded so that the silver crest embroidered on the pocket gleamed in the darkness.

'Algy's blazer,' Sid shouted, and leapt for the ladder, Rosie behind him. I swarmed up next, then Clio. Then we were on the cinder path, running so fast that my teeth jolted. A train went by below it, shaking the earth. I passed Sid and Rosie and a dark shape passed me: Jake, frisking his legs like a puppy. 'Find 'em boy,' I cried, and Jake stopped so suddenly that I nearly fell over him. 'He's no *use*,' Sid gasped. 'Only for *tricks*. He's just a sort of circus dog, my uncle's trained him. How else d'you think he got up that ladder?'

We ran on. Trees went by like running shadows and the curved moon moved behind them. We came down to the river, flowing black and shiny out of the tunnel under Death Wall and racing fast to the boiling white froth of the weir. Rosie called 'Algy . . .' But there was no answer, only her voice echoing.

There was no way across the river here except at the far end of the tunnel before it narrowed down to the culvert. At this point, a series of concrete beams which were part of the supports of Death Wall, ran across the river from side to side. They were safe enough to walk over in daylight, but dangerous in the dark.

And it looked very black in the tunnel.

'Could they have got through into the site?' Clio said softly.

I shook my head. You could only get through the culvert in summer, when the river was low. Sid and I had done it once, lying flat in a canoe.

Clio said, 'When will your uncle come, Sid?'

'He'll phone the police first . . .' Sid looked at me. 'The girls better stay here to wait for him. We'll go into the tunnel.' He fished in his pocket and brought out a box of matches. There were only two inside.

'I haven't any,' I whispered.

He closed the box. 'Then we'll have to be careful.' I could see his face in the moonlight and knew he was horribly afraid. It made my heart turn over. We had to go into that black tunnel, on our own, not knowing what we would find there . . .

Then I had an idea. 'Jake,' I said, and beside me the huge dog pricked up his ears. 'Tricks are *some* use, Sid. If Algy's in the tunnel, Jake could sniff him out, couldn't he?'

Hope came into Sid's face, then went, like turning off a light. 'We haven't got anything of his. We should have picked up his blazer.'

'Clio's got his hanky,' I said. 'He gave it her when she was crying. In Lilac Lodge. Have you still got it, Clio?'

Looking slightly puzzled, because of course she didn't know about Jake and his tricks, she produced it out of her jersey sleeve.

'It'll smell of *her*, won't it?'

Sid pulled a face. 'Of Algy too, though. He might do it, it's just a bit harder. Here—give it to me.' He held the hanky to Jake who sniffed it and wagged his tail. 'Choccy,' Sid said, rather contemptuously, and dropped the handkerchief. Jake picked it up and ran round in a circle, nose to ground. He stopped at Clio, then jerked his great head up in the air like a horse jibbing at a gate, and started trotting round in a circle again.

'Stupid good-for-nothing dog,' Sid said between his teeth.

Suddenly Jake stopped circling and made a brisk bee-line

for the tunnel. We ran after him. The tunnel was dark; we edged along, keeping one hand on the wall. At first we could hear nothing except the silky sound of the water sliding past and then, ahead in the darkness, Jake began to whine.

'Strike a match,' I whispered. Sid was breathing quickly and unevenly. I heard the rasp as he opened the box. He gave a little grunt, and the match flared.

There was Jake—first Jake himself, creeping slowly along a concrete beam over the river, and then his enormous shadow beyond him, a hunched, monstrous beast against the sloping underside of Death Wall. And, across the river, huddling against the damp, green side of the tunnel, Mr Gribble and Algy. Mr Gribble was holding Algy in front of him, one arm locked round his neck. Algy's eyes were closed, he looked dead. Mr Gribble was staring at Jake.

Sid gave a squeak as the match burned his fingers. He dropped it and it hissed in the river.

'Call off your dog,' Mr Gribble's voice echoed like a horn in the tunnel.

Sid lit his second match. Mr Gribble edged along the side of the tunnel, dragging Algy with him. His eyes were fixed on the dog. Jake was moving closer, his belly almost brushing the beam. 'Call him off,' Mr Gribble said, in a voice suddenly thick with fear. If we had not been frightened for Algy, it would have been funny—the cowering man and the huge, silly, playful, circus dog, who would do nothing when he reached the other side except drop the handkerchief at Algy's feet and wait for a chocolate . . .

But Mr Gribble did not know that. And Jake did look terrifying—not only huge but *strange*, for what ordinary dog would balance on that concrete beam? He must have looked to Mr Gribble like some creature out of a nightmare. 'Call him off at once,' he cried, 'Or I'll throw the boy in the river . . .'

Sid caught his breath. 'Jake, Jake . . .' Jake wagged his tail in reply. 'He can't *get* back, he can't go backwards,' Sid said, horrified. He shouted, 'It's all right, he won't hurt you, really he won't . . .'

'He wouldn't hurt a fly,' I cried.

Our voices boomed back from the walls of the tunnel.

'*Call him off.*' Mr Gribble's face was twisted—demented with terror. The bank on the other side was narrow: he and Algy were very close to the edge.

The second match went out. Yellow spots danced in front of my eyes in the blackness. I thought of Aristotle, whirling along in the current and breaking into pieces on the posts of the weir. 'Don't throw him in, he'll drown,' I shrieked, and then, in desperation, 'Jake—Jake, good boy, come back . . .'

There was a splash, like a log hitting the water. Sid cried out, '*Algy,*' and we stumbled back to the mouth of the tunnel. My heart was in my mouth. Sid couldn't swim, so it was up to me. But though I had my Life Saver's Badge, I wouldn't stand a chance in that current. We would be drowned, Algy and I . . .

Sobbing under my breath, I struggled out of my blazer as I ran, and, as we came out of the tunnel, bent to tug off my shoes.

There was a dark shape in the middle of the river. I flung back my arms to do a flat dive and Sid caught my wrist and held me. 'It's all right . . . it's Jake . . . look . . .'

He was battling along, head high. He struggled to the opposite bank, climbed out, shook himself, and bounced back, barking gaily, into the tunnel. As Uncle William and the Jamaican porter came running down to the river, Mr Gribble began screaming.

His screams had subsided to moans by the time the police arrived—two constables and the Inspector. By then, Uncle William and the porter had brought Algy to safety, edging carefully over the beam like a pair of outsize acrobats while Sid held the porter's hurricane lamp high and Mr Gribble lay on the far bank like a bundle of old clothes someone had thrown out for the dustman. All Jake had done was lick his face, but it had made him paralysed with fear. The police brought handcuffs with them. 'A stretcher would have been more to the point,' Uncle William said.

They needed a stretcher for Algy. While they fetched it, he lay on the bank by the river with my blazer under his head and Uncle William's hairy overcoat covering him. His glasses were broken, he was covered in dirt and blood and there was a great weal coming up one side of his face, but he was alive.

'His poor *face*,' Rosie sobbed, as we crouched beside him.

Algy opened his eyes. 'He kicked me in the face when I went up the ladder, but I went on running . . .' His voice was sliding and dreamy. 'Then . . . in the tunnel I followed him across the beam . . . he started thumping me . . . did you find my blazer? . . . My head hurts . . .'

'Don't talk,' the Inspector said. 'You'll soon be home. Just as soon as the doctor's had a look at you.'

'I don't want to go home,' Algy said. 'Oh please . . . please . . . I don't want to go home . . .' He began to cry weakly. The tears spurted out of his eyes and mixed with the dirt and blood on his face. 'I don't want to go home . . . I don't want to go home . . .' Rosie and Clio began to cry in sympathy and I felt a great lump come up in my throat.

'What's all this about?' the Inspector said, in an astonished voice.

He was looking at me. And a little later on, when we were following the stretcher back to the station yard, I walked beside him and told him.

CHAPTER TWELVE

CHAMPAGNE FOR A HANDFUL OF THIEVES

'We've been looking for him a long time,' the Inspector said when he called round early on Saturday morning before Mum had time to tidy the sitting-room. Although she pretended to be sitting quietly and listening to the Inspector, I could see her eyes darting round as she worried about the dust.

'Gribble—Hubbel—his real name is Joshua Green,' the Inspector went on. 'He's made what you might call a speciality of old ladies. Lodged with them for a couple of weeks, sometimes taking a job nearby, sometimes not. Robbed them of their savings and then disappeared into thin air . . .'

'But Sid's uncle asked if you knew about anyone like him,' I said. 'It ought to have been *easy*. With him being a vegetarian!'

The Inspector smiled. 'He's no more a vegetarian than I am! It wasn't just his name he changed each time. Once he pretended to be a Baptist Minister—sang hymns in the bathroom and said long prayers before meals. That particular lady complained that her dinner always got cold on her plate but she didn't like to mention it, in case she upset him. Another time he was a sailor. Spent all his time splicing rope and doing fancy knots. He was very thorough at disguising himself, you see, and there was a reason behind it. It meant that there was always something special about him that his victims would remember, and as it was always different each time, it was hard for us to track him down.'

'A bit of an artist in his way,' Dad said.

'An actor,' the Inspector said. 'Matter of fact, that's what he used to be before he decided that robbing old people was an easier living. He's a nasty customer. We know about six old age pensioners he's stolen from and there may be a lot more we don't know about. People like Mrs Blackadder, who're too proud to admit they've been taken in!'

'I can't think why Mother didn't tell me,' my Mum cried.

The Inspector gave a little cough. 'Perhaps she didn't want to upset you. Anyway, we've got him at last—that's what matters. Thanks to young Fred and his friends.' He glanced at me and added hastily, 'Though what they *did* was wrong, of course. I hope they'll remember in future that there are some things even the police aren't allowed to do in this country. We've decided to overlook their behaviour, but we might not another time! No more breaking and entering, young man!'

'I should hope not,' Mum said indignantly. 'Why, Fred might have been hurt, like that poor boy Algy Beecham! Is he going to be all right?'

'Out of hospital this morning. They only kept him in for one night. He'd been knocked about a bit but nothing serious. No bones broken. More shock than anything.'

I drew a deep breath. 'What about his parents?'

The Inspector looked at me. 'Hmm. Well, as a matter of fact I had a talk with them at the hospital. Bearing in mind what you'd told me. They're not cruel people, you know Fred, just a bit over-anxious, too ambitious, perhaps. They expect too much, that's hard on a sensitive boy.'

This wasn't what I wanted to know. 'But what did they *say*? Are they angry? Algy said last night that he'd rather be *dead* . . .'

'I don't think you need worry.' Suddenly the Inspector's eyes were twinkling. 'I took the opportunity of telling them what a brave lad he was, almost a hero. Clever, too. Tracking a thief down, tackling him single-handed . . .'

I struggled with myself. 'He didn't do it *all*,' I couldn't help saying. 'Just the last bit.'

'Perhaps I did lay it on a bit thick. But in a good cause, it seemed to me. His parents were pretty impressed by the time I'd finished. His father said he didn't think he had it in him!' The Inspector chuckled. 'I should think that boy's going to find life a bit easier, from now on.'

He looked at my Mum who was gazing longingly at the vacuum cleaner, which was standing by the door with a duster and a tin of polish beside it. He cleared his throat. 'I'd better be going now. I'm afraid I came a bit early and interrupted your housework, Mrs McAlpine.'

'There's no time of the day you wouldn't do that,' Dad said.

Mum looked a little embarrassed and to show she really had been interested and paying attention, she said, 'Is there any chance my mother will get her money back?'

'I rather doubt it. Of course we'll do what we can, but he may well have spent most of it.'

'We're going to have a jumble sale for Gran, Sunday,' I said. 'I suppose you wouldn't like to buy a raffle ticket for a grand piano, would you?'

'A grand piano? Where'd you get a grand piano from?'

'Well, we haven't got it, exactly. But when Algy was collecting the jumble, he met a man who'd got one and wanted to get rid of it and he said anyone could have it if they'd take it away. So we thought we'd raffle it and the person who won would just have to go and collect it. It was Algy's idea.'

The Inspector said, 'I thought you told me Algy wasn't clever? That boy'll go a long way, mark my words.' He gave me a shilling for two tickets but he said he didn't really want a grand piano as he lived in a small house, so if he won he would be glad if we would just forget about it.

When he had gone, Dad said, 'Gran's got a few surprises coming to her, hasn't she? Matter of fact, she may have had one already. I met Puttock yesterday afternoon, on the way home.'

He wouldn't say anymore. He said it was Gran's surprise

and she would want to tell us herself. And then he sat, grinning to himself like a man with a secret, until Mum got annoyed and told him to clear out of the room so that she could get on with her cleaning.

I went round to Gran at once. She was sitting by the fire. In spite of last night's excitement, she looked about ten years younger and very cheerful. On the table beside her stood a bottle of her home-made wine and two glasses with dregs in them.

'Has Mr Puttock been?' I asked, dipping my finger in a glass to get out the last drop.

'Don't do that. Other people's germs. Yes, Mr Puttock's been. What's it to you?'

'Dad said there was a surprise.'

'Did he tell you what?'

'No. He said you'd want to. What is it, Gran?'

'Wait and see.' She looked at me teasingly. 'I tell you what, Fred, bring the others round to tea this afternoon and I'll tell you then. We'll have a party. As long as Algy's well enough, of course. We couldn't have a party without the hero, could we?'

I sighed a little. I was glad for Algy's sake that everyone was proud of him, but it seemed a bit hard that he should get all the glory. For a moment I wished Mr Gribble *had* thrown him in the river and I had plunged to the rescue. I wondered if I should tell Gran how I nearly had dived in, even though I knew I would probably drown, but instead I just said, 'He was jolly brave. Going after Mr Gribble alone like that.'

Gran smiled, not as if she found something funny, but gently and fondly as if she were suddenly pleased with me for some reason. 'Being brave is often a matter of getting a chance to be,' she said. 'But you were all brave, and kind-hearted and generous too, which in a lot of ways is more important. You might have got yourselves into serious trouble—and all for the sake of a foolish old woman who should have had the common sense to go to the police in the first place!'

I said, 'I'm rather glad you didn't, Gran. It wouldn't have been nearly such fun,' and this time she laughed until the tears came and held out her arms to me. 'Come and kiss me, Fred,' she said, 'and then take yourself off. I've got a lot to do, getting ready for this old party.'

Algy's mother drove him to Gran's that afternoon. She wouldn't come in, but when I heard the car I went out and she gave me a long parcel and told me to give it to Gran and asked what time she should come for Algy. 'The doctor says he ought to be in bed fairly early, but of course we don't want to break the party up.'

I said about six-thirty would probably be all right, and she helped Algy out of the car, as gently as if he were an egg that might break.

The parcel was a bottle of champagne. 'It's for after tea,' Algy said. He had a plaster on one cheek and a scarlet and orange bruise above his eye.

'You should have a bit of steak put on that,' Gran said.

'I think it looks beautiful, like a sunset. Don't you think so, Fred?' Clio said, and my sister Jinny nudged me.

'I thought you said she was awful,' she whispered, when we went out to fetch the jellies Gran had put to set in the wash-house.

'Oh she's not so bad sometimes. When you get to know her.' I was rather surprised to hear myself saying this.

Jinny gave that irritating laugh older sisters give when they think they know something you don't. 'You ought to hear what she says about you, it 'ud make your ears burn,' she said. 'Fred this, Fred that—all the time we were laying the table!'

'She's just a nut case,' I said, and marched back into the room with the jelly.

Clio had arrived early and helped Jinny and Gran get the party ready. Gran had got out her best lace cloth but you could hardly see it because of all the food. There was apple pie and cream, and meringues and cream, and chocolate éclairs, and honey crunch biscuits, and ginger nuts, and jelly and a huge plate of sliced ham with tomatoes round it, cut so they fell open like water lilies. And oranges and nuts and a box of chocolate drops for Jake.

Uncle William said he would leave the dog outside in the van, but Gran insisted he came in. 'Just room for another little one,' she said, when Uncle William had taken off his overcoat and Jake had stretched out by the fire. 'Where's Rosie?'

I looked at the clock. 'She ought to be here now. You did tell her, Sid?'

Sid nodded. 'She said she'd got something to do, she didn't say what, only that she'd be here by four.'

It was after that now. 'We'll wait till half-past,' Gran said.

The loaded table and Uncle William and Jake took up most of the room, the rest of us squashed in where we could. We had cleared a space and made a pile of socks and ties and shoes, so that Gran could see Jake's trick of returning things to their owners, when Rosie knocked at the door. She had old Puffer with her.

'I brought Mr FitzWilliam, do you mind, Mrs Blackadder? I went down to the site to fetch the jumble and he wasn't there so I went to Lilac Lodge. I wanted to tell him—well, I just wanted to say we were sorry we'd been beastly to him, and he was sitting in his room not working because of his cough. His room's horribly cold, like an ice box, and I thought you wouldn't mind if I asked him to the party too.'

'Bit of an intrusion,' old Puffer wheezed, 'but the young lady insisted.' His pale, papery face looked surprised, as if he wasn't quite sure how he had got here. 'Wouldn't take no for an answer,' he said in an astonished voice, and Sid winked at me: we had often wondered how Rosie's lame ducks felt about *being* lame ducks.

'I'm glad she did,' Gran said. 'Sit down, Mr FitzWilliam, and I'll get some lemon and honey for that cough. What jumble, Rosie?'

'Don't tell her,' the rest of us shouted in chorus.

Gran looked at us. 'Why not? If you don't, I won't tell you *my* surprise. Come on now, fair's fair.'

'Well, it's for a sale,' I said, and explained about the jumble and the raffle tickets, not because of what she'd said about her secret—she was only teasing about that—but because I thought this party was probably costing a lot and it would ease her mind to know there would soon be some money to help pay for it.

Gran listened but she didn't smile and I remembered that she didn't like talking about money or people knowing she was poor, and I wondered if she was cross with us. Then I saw her eyes were soft and shining and I knew she wasn't.

'You're kind children,' she said. 'Very kind.' For a minute she looked almost sad enough to cry, then she brightened up and smiled at us all. 'But as far as money goes—well, things aren't as bad as all that! And that's my surprise! A dealer came to see Mr Puttock the other day and offered him quite a lot of money for Albert's old picture. Three hundred and fifty pounds. Mr Puttock said you could have knocked him down with a feather! He'd given Mr Gribble five pounds for it, and reckoned it would fetch about ten. It's by a painter called Muggs. Henry Muggs. Not a very good painter, you know, too pretty-pretty, and until a few years ago that picture wouldn't have been worth twopence. Certainly it wasn't worth anything when Albert died. But fashions change and apparently Mr Muggs is quite highly thought of now. Only by people who don't know any better, if you want *my* opinion, but I suppose that's beside the point.'

'But Gran,' I said. 'Doesn't the picture belong to Mr Puttock? I mean, he bought it.'

'*Thought* he'd bought it,' Sid said. 'It was stolen, so it wasn't really his, was it?'

'That's beside the point, too,' Gran said. 'Because Mr Puttock came round this morning to tell me he wanted me to have the money. For old times sake, he said, I'd been good to him in the past.' She beamed on us all. 'So I'm a rich woman now. You can all get round my table and tuck in and no holds barred!'

We all sat round the table somehow, except old Puffer who sat in the armchair by the fire with Jake at his feet, and drank hot lemon and honey. We asked Gran what she was going to do with the money and she looked mysterious and said she had a few ideas about that but she didn't want to discuss them just yet. And then she asked us to tell her everything that had happened. Though she had a rough idea, she said, there must be a lot of bits she had missed. We were only too happy to oblige: we all began talking at once, so loud and so fast that Gran put her hands over her ears.

'One at a time, *please*,' she begged.

'Let Fred tell it,' Clio said. 'He's best at explaining things.'

Sid looked rather sour at this, because he always comes top in English, but the others agreed so I began at the beginning, when we had seen Mr Gribble arriving at Gran's door and Sid had said he was sinister. I put everything in, even about how we had lost Aristotle, and old Puffer wheezed and chuckled by the fire and said he had been mad at the time but now he could see the funny side. The others were quiet at first but by the time I got to the burglary at Lilac Lodge they couldn't help chipping in, and Gran didn't stop them but did her best to listen to us all. She laughed and laughed when we told her about Mr Stanley's false teeth grinning away in the glass; but later on, when we got to the part where Mr Gribble had Algy trapped in the tunnel and was threatening to throw him in the river, she began to look frightened. 'And then our last match went out,' Sid said, 'and there was this awful *splash* and Fred thought it was Algy. And d'you know, he near as damn-it *dived in*—had his blazer and shoes off and if I hadn't stopped him he'd have gone in and he'd have been drowned, the stupid, half-witted fool . . .'

Across the table, Gran's eyes met mine. 'You didn't tell me that, Fred.'

'Oh, Fred doesn't ever boast,' Algy said.

While we had been talking the tea had all vanished, except for a few crumbs, and when our stomachs had settled, just before six o'clock, Uncle William opened the champagne. The cork oozed out slowly between his great thumbs and then suddenly shot to the ceiling with a sound like an air-gun. The champagne frothed out and Gran held a cup ready because the glasses she had for her home-made wine were too small. So we washed out our tea cups and put the champagne in them.

'A toast,' Sid said, clambering on his chair. 'A toast to our charming hostess, Mrs Edwina Blackadder.' He rolled his eyes. 'Without whose help we would never have entered on a life of crime!'

Gran laughed and we sipped our champagne. Clio laughed because the bubbles went up her nose and Uncle William smacked his lips and said, 'This is the stuff to give the troops,' and roared with laughter too.

They were all laughing, all my friends and my Gran and Sid's Uncle William and old Puffer; even Jake was thumping his tail on the hearthrug. We were all so happy that I had an ache in my chest that was almost like sadness. I felt happy and sad at the same time and very fond of everybody.

Gran rapped a spoon on the table. 'Now *I* must propose a toast. What shall I say? To my friends and benefactors?'

'To the Committee,' we cried.

'The Thieves' Committee,' Clio said, red in the face with giggling.

Uncle William shook his head. 'I don't like that. A Committee sounds too respectable for a lot of burglars. *I* know. There are five of you, five makes a handful. What about a handful of thieves?'

'To a handful of thieves, then.' Gran lifted her cup and drank.

'That would make a lovely title for a book,' Jinny said.

And this is the end of my story. Not the real end, of course, because things went on happening after the champagne was drunk and the party was over: Clio's mother and father are home now and Rosie's mother has had another baby, and Algy's parents are—well—not *perfect* but better, and though my Mum and Gran are still arguing, they seem to enjoy it. And Gran is much better off than she used to be, not just because of the three hundred and fifty pounds but because old Puffer—I can't get used to calling him Mr FitzWilliam—lives with her now and they've turned the wash-house into a work-shop and he works there, framing pictures for Mr Puttock. There's a new night watchman on the site but we don't see much of him, because although we still go down to Death Wall sometimes, we go less often than we used to.

Jinny says stories ought to end with people getting married and living happily ever after, but we are too young for that. So as you have to end a book somewhere, this seems as good a place as any. All of us at a party, and all of us happy.

Printed in Great Britain
by Amazon.co.uk, Ltd.,
Marston Gate.